TOMORROW'S TEARS

ELEANOR JONES

TOMORROW'S TEARS

Copyright: © 2010 by Eleanor Jones
Original title: Tomorrow's Tears
Cover illustration: © Jennifer Bell
Cover layout: Stabenfeldt AS

Typeset by Roberta L. Melzl
Editor: Bobbic Chasc
Printed in Germany, 2010

ISBN: 978-1-934983-67-6

Stabenfeldt Inc.
225 Park Avenue South
New York, NY 10003
www.pony.us

Available exclusively through PONY.

CHAPTER 1

The mind-blowing, special moment of total connection lasted for a second that seemed like a lifetime. A touch of the calves, a thought, a suggestion; unwritten signs, tentatively controlling the awesome power of muscle and sinew so that horse and rider moved as one, each totally in touch with the spirit of freedom for a glorious moment in time...

The explosion was inevitable; one huge backbreaking buck that dislodged with ease the slightly built girl from her dream. Disappointment flooded in, larger than fear, as she begrudgingly parted with the most magnificent horse she had ever sat upon. And as the ground came suddenly to meet her she let herself go limp, clinging to the magical memory... for the moment *had* been there, so surely it would come again.

Cassie sat squarely on the muddy ground, glaring reproachfully at the large bay gelding that towered over her, a dull ache slowly spreading across her backside to match the painful dent to her pride. It had been such an awesome experience, though, that she could never regret it.

Cosmic, her mount of two seconds ago, stared back disdainfully, blowing down his nostrils and snorting loudly, his perfect white star a hazy blur as he tossed his elegant head.

"I'm sure he has a smile on his face," she groaned, putting her face in her hands.

Silas Wiggins, head groom at Hope Bank Stables, reached out a gnarled hand to help her up. "You can't blame the horse, missy," he told her. "You should never have tried to ride him today; he's been off work for a week with that abscess, and even in the best of times he's not the easiest."

Cassie clambered to her feet, glancing woefully up at the old man as she tried to brush the telltale mud from her well-worn blue jodhpurs. "Robert is going to kill me, isn't he?"

Silas's leathery face crinkled into a broad grin, his blue eyes twinkling. "Only if he finds out."

Cassie returned his conspiratorial smile with a rush of gratitude, already reaching for the horse's rein. "Come on, then," she announced, ignoring the fluttering feeling in her chest. "I suppose I'd better try again."

"Cassie Truman," grumbled Silas, in a tone that disguised his admiration of the determined teenager. "Do you never learn?"

"Well, you taught me," she retaliated. "Never give up, you always say, so…"

He took the rein from her, shaking his head slowly from side to side before gesturing in the direction of the barn. "Well… if you're sure you're alright. Go and get the lunge line and whip then; I'll get the edge off him for you first."

Cassie stepped into the fragrance of the long barn, pausing for a moment, as always, to take a breath. She could never seem to get enough of the familiar smell; hay, leather, manure and sweat; so many scents all rolled into one delicious aroma that just spelled horse. What would it be like to actually live here, she wondered, to wake up every morning, as her best friend Laura did, and walk straight out of the house into the stable yard?

A dozen heads turned in her direction, whickering gently. "It's not feeding time yet, guys," she told them, reaching up onto the rack for the lunge line and selecting a long whip from the box in the corner. "And as for you, Bobby…"

She reached down to wrap her arms around the shaggy neck of Hope Bank's mascot; an ancient Shetland pony that Robert Ashton had ridden as a child.

6

"He's been around for so long that he deserves the right to do exactly what he wants," Robert always insisted when Mollie, his wife and joint owner of Hope Bank Stables, tried to persuade him to keep his old friend under better control. She too thought the world of Bobby, but he drove her mad at times – especially when he managed to find his way into the house where, on more than one occasion, he'd been caught, calmly eating the plants in the hallway.

Nothing, however, could sway Robert from his total adoration of the cheeky chestnut; in his eyes, the little guy could do no wrong. His sixteen-year-old daughter, Laura, liked to declare to whoever would listen that Bobby was her dad's one and only weakness, a chink in his otherwise formidable armor.

Everyone else at Hope Bank – horses, dogs *and* people – had to earn their keep, including Steel, the dark gray youngster that Laura rode in competitions. She lived in constant fear that one day her dad would calmly announce that he had received an offer for the horse that was just too good to be true. In fact, it was only because of her mother's intervention that he hadn't already done so.

Almost as if reading Cassie's thoughts, Steel reached out from his corner box at that exact moment to nibble her arm. She fumbled in her pocket for a grubby piece of carrot and he took it gently, reflecting his sweet personality. Poor Laura, thought Cass, struggling to fend off Bobby's more pushy advances, everyone thought that she had all the advantages. Both her parents had been successful show jumpers and there was a constant stream of talented horses passing through Hope Bank for her to ride, so it seemed, in a way, that she really did have every opportunity to do well. The reality, however, was that she was expected to work incredibly hard around the stables, and every time she started to make real headway with a horse, it had to be sold.

"This is a business, and we are in it to make money," was her father's practical explanation when she'd objected wildly. "You'll just have to get used to it, I'm afraid."

Where Bobby was concerned, though, he seemed to have a blind spot. "You don't know how lucky you are," Cassie told the tiny chestnut when he nudged her firmly, demanding a treat. "And I'm shutting you in the barn now, whether you like it or not. I've got enough problems without you distracting Cosmic."

She hurried back out into the bright morning sunshine, sliding the bolt carefully on the barn door before turning around to see Robert Ashton's tall familiar figure. He was leaning forward, talking earnestly to Silas, his prematurely gray head bobbing up and down with excitement or anger. Her heart thumped into her boots; Robert had distinctly told her not to ride Cosmic but, as usual, she had been unable to resist trying to prove something. And who was she kidding, anyway? No matter how well she rode, Robert would never let a fifteen-year-old jump one of his youngsters. Laura helped school most of the horses, but even she only got to actually compete with Steel. Apart from Robert himself, it was always the impudent, outspoken charmer, Jack Delaney, who took all the glory – when he actually came to work, that was. Unless it was a show day they could never really rely on him, but today was an exception. This morning, to everyone's surprise, he'd turned up first thing with his usual broad grin and offered to spray the weeds in the Long Meadow.

Silas gave Cassie an exaggerated wink as she approached the two men, and her breathing became easier.

9

"Hi, Rob," she called brightly. "I thought you and Mollie weren't back until this afternoon."

"The lots went through sooner than we thought," he responded, "and both of the four-year-olds we were interested in were way too expensive, so we thought we'd head back early."

He tuned to look at Cosmic, and ran a practiced hand down the horse's fine boned fore leg. "Anyway, Cos' seems fine now, so Silas is going to get the high sprits out of him on the lunge and then…" He cast the old man a concerned frown. "… I'm busy, Jack has to leave early, and Laura has gone to the dentist, so Silas seems to think that you will be able to ride him."

Cassie dropped the lunge equipment in her excitement, clasping her hands together. "Yes, oh yes… I'm sure I can. Thank you!"

Robert glared at her. "Well, don't you dare fall off or you'll have me to answer to. He's doing well, and I don't want him learning any bad habits."

As he strode off she caught Silas's eye. "You won't fall off, will you?" he asked.

"Of course not," she smiled.

Silas expertly looped the lunge line around his hand, clipped the end of it onto the ring on Cosmic's cavesson and brought his whip around from beneath his arm, the end of it trailing on the ground.

"Walk on," he ordered, clicking loudly. The big bay gelding tossed his head, breaking immediately into trot.

"Steady…. Steady, boy," he crooned, but Cosmic seemed totally oblivious to his handler's commands. He burst into canter, leaping and bucking while Silas held on determinedly, playing the horse like a fish on a line.

"You see," he called to Cassie, who was watching wide-eyed. "All these high spirits have to be released. I'll just let him buck and play a bit and then you can get on."

Cassie clenched her fists, her mouth becoming dry at the thought of actually mounting the huge explosive animal. It was no wonder that after that first two minutes of amazing connection he had bucked her right off. What had she been thinking, trying to ride him in the first place? It had just seemed too good an opportunity to miss, though, with everyone away for the morning, and Cosmic looking so eager to get out. She hadn't thought about the fact that he'd been cooped up in his stable for a week. What an idiot she was.

"Unless you've changed your mind?" grinned Silas.

Cassie jumped off the fence, her small frame growing in stature as she threw back her shoulders determinedly. "Of course I haven't," she insisted. "I'm looking forward to it."

Cosmic slowed down, listening now to Silas's crooning tones, his rib cage rising and falling with each heaving breath.

"Well, don't you dare fall off," grumbled Silas. "Or Rob really will have something to say."

"Yes," grinned Cassie. "But not because he's bothered by the thought of me hurting myself."

Cosmic came to a halt, lowering his head to push against Silas. The elderly groom ran a practiced hand down the horse's face, rubbing him gently on his perfect white star. "Of course not," he smiled. "He just doesn't want the horse to learn that he can buck people off, that's all. In a way I suppose you might say that the whole thing is just a con anyway, but we certainly can't afford for them to learn bad habits."

Cassie walked across to join him. "What do you mean? What's a con?"

"Us, handling horses. They're all stronger than any man,

11

but we train them to *believe* that we're in charge, so their natural instincts adapt."

"You mean, the natural instinct to fit in, on the pecking order of the herd?"

"Got that right," responded Silas, letting down the stirrups. "They're flight animals, nervous creatures that need guidance. We just have to win their trust and make sure that we're well up on their pecking order; *then* they'll believe that we're in charge and, hopefully, do as we ask. Anyway, come on, and let's hope that Cos' here hasn't decided that you're somewhere near the bottom of his."

To Cass's dismay, just as she put her foot into the stirrup, Jack suddenly appeared. "Are you sure about this?" he grinned, resting his arms on the gate as if intending to watch her progress.

She glanced nervously across at him, settling herself down into the saddle. "I thought you had to go home early," she retorted.

His dark eyes sparkled. "Oh, I guess I can stick around for a while; I certainly wouldn't want to miss this."

"If Rob realizes that you're still here then he'll make *you* ride him, you know," remarked Silas.

Jack laughed, already slouching off toward the barn. "I get your point. Give me a shout if you need a hand picking her up, though."

To Cass's relief, her second ride on the big bay had none of the explosiveness of the first.

She sat down quietly, feeling for her right stirrup and taking up the reins with tense fingers. "Now, don't let him feel that you're nervous," advised Silas, "or you'll really be in trouble."

Her objection was immediate. "I'm not nervous," she insisted, asking Cosmic to step forward.

The elegant bay gelding was everything she had felt before and yet so much more. The perfect line of communication was still there, as if they really were both on the same wavelength. With a touch of her calf they were going sideways; with a shift of her shoulders he turned.

"When you want to slow down just sit up," called Silas. "Take sitting trot, open your shoulders and pull up from the base of your stomach."

Cassie did as she was told and the horse responded magically. "He's awesome," she cried.

"So you really can ride him," cut in Robert Ashton's voice.

She glanced across to see him leaning against the fence and hot color flooded her face. "He's the best horse I've ever ridden."

"Or are ever likely to," smiled Robert. "Just have a canter and that will do for today. I have someone coming to see him tomorrow."

A heavy lump suddenly found its way into Cassie's chest, taking away her pleasure at the big horse's huge canter stride. She did one circle and pulled up, anger rising inside her in an all-engulfing tide. "But you can't sell him," she exclaimed, the color in her cheeks concentrated into two bright spots.

"It's what he's here for," explained Robert with surprising sympathy. "You can ask Laura. We bring them on, develop their skills and sell them for a hefty profit. That's the business. This guy will be the top of the line in dressage, you mark my words, and I'll bet you see him in *Horse and Rider* in a couple of years."

"It's the ones with no talent you should feel sorry for," added Silas. "Or the difficult ones; who knows where they end up. This guy, now…" He took the horse's rein as she slid to the ground. "… This guy will have the best of everything."

It was almost five thirty by the time all the chores had been finished and Cassie was ready to head home. She paused at the gate to look back across the small quadrangle of stone stables that formed the original yard, behind which was the new barn. A warm glow flooded her at the sight of all the contented horses, nibbling happily on their bulging hay nets.

"It's a good sight, isn't it?" remarked Jack, appearing from nowhere, as usual. He stopped beside her, silent for once, as if, surprisingly, in total attunement with her emotions. "To see them all settled for the night is something special; even that new horse seems to have gotten over his nerves. I'll miss this place when I'm gone."

Cass turned in surprise, looking up to catch the sudden shadow that flashed across his face. "Gone?" she cried. "Gone where? Are you leaving?"

He laughed then, his usual lighthearted, devil-may-care laugh. "Who knows? There's far too much to see in this world, though, to stay around in one place for long."

"It seems to me that nothing ever stays the same for long around here," grumbled Cass. "You're going away now, and look at Cosmic; I just can't believe that Rob's going to sell him."

Jack shrugged. "Well, that is what he's here for," he reminded her. "What most of the horses are here for, come to think of it. We just have to do the best we can for them while they're here, and hope that they go on to bigger and better things."

"Yes," agreed Cass. "But we keep Bobby, and he's no good to anyone."

Jack laughed. "Now that's a totally different story. In a way, I suppose he shows that even Rob has a hidden soft spot."

"A very odd one, if you ask me," she retorted.

The tiny Shetland appeared just then, almost as if on cue, trotting eagerly toward them from around the corner. "The little horror escaped from the field again," roared Jack, trying to grab his long mane before he disappeared into the feed room.

"I'll go and get a head collar," laughed Cass, running off toward the barn.

By the time Cass eventually set off for home again the shadows were lengthening, making strange shapes on the ground. She jumped in and out of them as she jogged along the road, smiling to herself at the memory of Bobby, digging in his hooves and refusing to return to his field while Jack pulled helplessly on his lead rope.

Robert Ashton came running from the office, alerted by the noise, and she and Robert both doubled over with laughter at poor Jack, whose face was getting redder by the minute.

"Call yourself a horseman?" Robert had said, holding out his hand. "Here, give him to me."

When Jack begrudgingly handed over the lead rope, Rob just patted Bobby's mud-encrusted neck. "Poor boy," he murmured. "Are these horrid people bothering you?"

Bobby whickered in response, tossing his head, and proceeded to sweetly follow the tall gray-haired man back across the yard.

"Would you like me to give you some lessons?" laughed Rob, looking across at Jack.

Cass burst into a fit of giggles while Jack cursed under

15

his breath. "Yes," he remarked, cheering up. "Look where he's taking him, though."

"Well, it's no wonder that Bobby listens to Rob," Cass cried as they watched the barn door open.

"Gives in to his every whim," agreed Jack, his dark eyes suddenly crinkling at the corners. Then he broke out laughing so hard she thought he might burst, standing in the center of the stable yard with his hands on his knees and tears streaming down his face. She would remember him like that, always.

The sun was low in the sky as Cass wandered homewards, casting a red glow across the meadow beside the road and outlining the wooded hillside ahead with a rim of gold. She sighed, a contented heartfelt sigh, bundling her unruly chestnut hair back into the confines of the elastic hair band while her mind wandered toward the future. Tomorrow she was going to the Tall Trees boarding stable at the other end of Braeburn to try out Anna Anderson's dappled gray cob, Duke, and she had a really strange feeling about it – as if it was meant to be. Was this the one, she wondered, the horse of her dreams?

For months now some instinct deep inside had been telling her that somewhere out there was a horse that would change her whole life and she just knew, without a shadow of doubt, that she was biding her time until it appeared. Maybe this was it, she thought with a shiver of anticipation, maybe tomorrow her premonition would be realized.

Apart from wanting to fulfill her dream of owning a special horse, Cass's passion to compete meant that she would always willingly take any mount she could get. Anna Anderson was nervous about jumping, so she had asked Cass to ride Duke in the novice class at the pony club show next weekend.

"You'll just make yourself look bad," Laura groaned when they had discussed it earlier that day. "The cob can't jump to save its life. Tell her you can't do it."

Cass, however, had been adamant, setting her jaw determinedly. "It doesn't matter," she'd insisted. "I'll ride anything if it gives me the chance to compete. Surely even a bad experience is better than no experience at all."

"Not if you don't get over the first fence," Laura had giggled. "Can you imagine the look on the estimable Estelle's face then?"

Cassie had just shrugged. "Why should I care what she thinks? Just because her dad's loaded and she can buy the best horses doesn't make her a good rider. At least I'll have a varied experience."

"Various rides on seriously bad horses, you mean," Laura had reminded her, grimacing. "Although I do see what you're saying. All Estelle needs to do is steer, and both her horses just take her around the course."

Cass thought about their conversation as she headed down the road toward the row of tiny terraced cottages that she called home. Her grandmother would be waiting with supper in the oven, keeping an eye out for her return, while Granddad Bill puttered around. Living with grandparents had some advantages, she decided; at least they were always there for you, even if they didn't have two pennies to rub together. What would it have been like if her parents were still alive, she found herself wondering. She had been almost too young to remember their car crash. It was all just a blur of tears and misery now, hours of emptiness, fear and confusion. Maybe they wouldn't even have lived here in Braeburn; maybe she would have had to live in a city! She increased her pace, mortified by the idea.

❀ ❀ ❀ ❀ ❀

The evening sun lit up the terraced, whitewashed cottages at the edge of the road, bringing a sparkle to the small square windows on either side of the neat front doors. They were like faces, she decided; like a row of friendly faces welcoming her home. And there was her grandmother, peering out anxiously, wondering and worrying.

A warm glow spread through her limbs like liquid honey; there was far more to life than money, she decided. Estelle Morgan could keep her fancy horses, and if Duke stopped at the first fence, so what! At least she'd gain a little experience. An involuntary smile curled her lips as she remembered Lucy Locket, Jenny Mullin's bright chestnut part-bred Arab filly. When Jenny sprained her ankle a month or so ago she'd asked Cass to ride the horse in a dressage competition she'd been entered in. After first refusing to enter the arena, Lucy had reared bolt upright with her in front of the judge, and they'd ended up being disqualified. Okay, she decided, so maybe all her experiences weren't that good, but surely she would get a break eventually, if she persevered for long enough. Maybe one day someone would actually ask her to ride a really talented horse, and then she and her new partner would be on their way to the top.

Her ever-present dream slipped to the back of her mind as the front door of the end cottage opened. "Come on, hon," called her grandmother. "Dinner's on the table."

Happily she did as she was told, her thoughts returning to the upcoming show as she raced up the stairs. Excitement kicked in. Maybe this was it. Maybe Duke would be better than Laura thought. Well… only one way to find out… Suddenly tomorrow beckoned enticingly.

CHAPTER 2

Tall Trees boarding stable was nestled beneath the awesome
sweep of the upper pasture that loomed toward the skyline,
its cluster of mismatched buildings appearing to have been
placed with no apparent concern for any kind of orderliness.
Cass stopped in the gateway, comparing it with the neat
uniformity of Hope Bank. Okay, so the stables may be a
bit of a hodgepodge, and they could have made an effort to
sweep the yard.

A small clump of hay swirled toward her in a mini
whirlwind, and piles of soiled bedding lay in heaps all the
way to the mountainous muckheap. She felt like taking a
brush and sweeping it up there, and she smiled to herself at
the thought. Old Silas was a stickler for tidiness and order
and it seemed that, despite herself, his example must have
rubbed off on her.

"Hi, are you looking for someone?"

The small fair-haired girl who appeared from what
was, presumably, the feed room, stopped in front of Cass,
depositing her two buckets with a thud and smiling up at
her with a wide-eyed friendliness.

Cassie hopped from foot to foot. "I'm looking for
Anna... Anna Anderson?"

"Ah..."

The girl raised her eyebrows. "... Then you must be
Cassandra Truman."

"Well... yes," Cassie said, her forehead puckering into a
frown. "Actually, it's just Cassie, but how did *you* know my
name?"

The girl laughed, picking up her buckets again. "Well,
you *are* taking on the impossible in trying to get that lump,

Duke, to jump, so I guess everyone around here has heard of you. Anna has been bragging all week about you taking him to the show."

Cassie's heart hit her boots with a hollow thud; well, there went her dream. "I'm going to do my best," she said gloomily. The girl set off across the untidy yard and she fell in beside her. "Is he that bad?"

"Actually..." The buckets were set on the ground again as the girl stopped to make a point. "He's a lazy pig who makes a regular monkey out of poor Anna. She can't even get him out of the yard on his own."

"Sounds like it's going to be fun, then...?"

"Charlotte," filled in the girl. "Well that's my real name, but most people just call me Charlie. Come on, I'll put these feeds in and then I'll introduce you to Duke."

"So Anna's not here?" responded Cass.

"She's never here," declared Charlie, dropping a bucket over the half door of an elegant looking Thoroughbred. "She just asked me to point you in the right direction... unless you've changed your mind?"

"Oh, no," insisted Cass, suddenly eager to see the monstrous Duke. "I like a challenge."

At first glance she was pleasantly surprised. The gray cob was overweight, which of course wasn't going to help his athleticism, but his eyes were kind and he pricked his exceptionally large ears when he saw her, nickering softly.

"Why," she announced, reaching over his door to run her hand down his face, "he's sweet."

"Until you try to get him to do something," remarked Charlie, pushing a stray strand of curly blonde hair back behind her ears. "Anyway, I'll leave you to get acquainted. The tack room is over there, if you decide to ride him."

❀ ❀ ❀ ❀ ❀

Cassie slipped into the stable, a small bubble of apprehension shortening her breath. "Are you going to make a fool out of me, boy?" she murmured.

When Duke realized that no more food was coming he lost interest in his visitor, turning his generous backside toward her and yanking a chunk of hay from his net with fierce determination.

Unperturbed, Cass walked over to his shoulder. "Well, I'm going to ride you, whether you like it or not," she told him, with a firm pat to his muscular neck. "So you may as well get used to the idea."

Charlie came back while Cass was saddling up, her bright, attractive face beaming over the door. "So you're going through with it?"

"He can't be that bad," insisted Cass. "Look at him, he's as gentle as a kitten."

"Big kitten," laughed Charlie. "Oh, and don't be surprised if the whole stable turns out to watch."

Cass fastened the girth tab, removing her head from beneath the saddle flap to look around with surprise. "But there's no one here."

"There will be," retorted Charlie with a knowing grin. Cassie's heart hit her boots with a thud.

The spectators slowly trickled in. "That's Mary," announced Charlie as Cass led Duke from his stable, nodding across toward a plump middle-aged woman wearing outrageous blue checked jodhpurs. "She has a big black and white hairy monster. And there's Kim..."

Cass stopped listening to her vivacious companion's continuous chatter about the people assembling in the yard, preferring to concentrate on the task at hand

21

and feeling more than a little disconcerted by all the attention.

"I'll take him in here first," she announced, leading the broad-chested gray determinedly across the untidy yard toward what appeared to be an outdoor schooling area.

"Want a leg up?" offered Charlie, already cupping her hand.

Cass slid down the stirrup and bent her knee. "Thanks, his saddle is sure to slip if I mount by the stirrup."

At first it seemed okay; the cob was a comfortable ride with generous strides and a decent front. Their first circuit around the school was a breeze, and Cass found herself smiling at the blur of interested faces; so much for Charlie's negativity, she decided happily.

It was when she asked for canter, however, that Duke's true mettle was tested. He picked up on the right leg, took one stride and suddenly she was flying through the air with the sound of half a dozen simultaneous intakes of breath in her ears. Automatically she closed her hand on the rein and waited for the thud, clinging on determinedly as the powerful cob headed for the gate. He may have managed to buck her off, but there was no way she was going to let him win.

For a moment she thought that he was going to drag her all the way back to his stable, heaving her limp body through the soft sand surface. Anger trickled in, slowly turning into a torrent. No! There was no way she was going to be made a fool of again. She pushed an elbow against the ground, anchoring herself, and called firmly. "Whoa, boy... whoa!"

When he stopped immediately it occurred to her that maybe big brash Duke was far more of a pussycat than he led everyone to believe; her confidence soared as she clambered to her feet with help from a red-faced Charlie.

"I'm so sorry," she cried, helping to brush Cass down. "I should have warned you that he does that, but…"

"But you thought that I seemed a bit cocky and wanted to knock me down a peg or two?"

Cassie's eyes crinkled with laughter, and as the corners of her lips curled, suddenly Charlie was smiling back at her. "Something like that," she chuckled. "And I really am sorry."

"Well, give me a leg up, then," urged Cass, already bending her knee to the nodding approval of the gathered spectators. "I really am going to have to prove something now."

Just as expected, it seemed that the wayward gray cob was far less determined than he had first appeared. As soon as he realized that his diminutive rider was not afraid to give him a sharp smack for misbehaving, he turned into an angel… until Cass relaxed, that is.

Two perfectly cantered figure eights, four strides of trot and a neat change of lead, rhythmic and smooth. Cass felt her whole body begin to glow as her seat swung along in total harmony with her mount's canter, watching from the corner of her eye as the spectators began slowly moving away, mumbling to each other and glancing back, appreciative of her progress. Only a couple of them noticed Duke's final attempt to outwit his rider.

It was as they passed the center of the school for the third time that the gray cob sensed Cassie's lapse in concentration. With the quickness of a cat he dropped a shoulder and turned sharply to the left, lurching her over to the right. Cass felt the wrench and tried to clamp her legs against him, grasping for the rein that had been yanked from her grip. Duke bunched his hindquarters as her fingers made contact. For an endless moment she hung, halfway between his powerful neck and the undulating ground

23

below, hauling with desperation. If he unseated her this time then she'd really be in trouble.

She heard Charlie's voice urging her on. "Hang on, Cass," and then suddenly she was back in the saddle, kicking on, around and around the school, determined to show her willful mount who was really the boss. When she finally allowed him to slow to a walk his sides were heaving. "Well, I think you've proved your point," remarked Charlie. "I don't think he'll be messing with you again anytime soon."

"It still doesn't mean that he'll jump though, does it?" responded Cass, thinking about tomorrow's show.

Charlie threw her a sympathetic grin. "Why don't you try him over a fence now?"

Cass shook her head. "There's no point. He's tired now, so it won't be a great success, and I'm not going to teach him anything in a few minutes. I'll just take my chance and go over the practice fence a few times tomorrow, when he's nice and fresh again."

"You're not bothered by the thought of him acting up again?"

In answer to Charlie's question Cass shrugged. "I'm counting on him feeling far too insecure away from home to mess with me tomorrow... anyway, I believe, or at least I hope, that I've made my point."

"It's too bad Anna wasn't here to see this," exclaimed a plump, pleasant-faced woman who'd watched the whole proceedings with interest.

"Hi, Mrs. Anderson," called Charlie. "Cass, meet Anna's mom."

On her way to Tall Trees early the next morning, Cass remembered the conversation that had followed and found herself feeling sorry for poor Anna Anderson, whose mother, though pleasant enough, appeared to have little understanding of her daughter's obvious fear of her own horse. Cass had tried to explain to her that, despite the fact that Mrs. A obviously adored him, maybe the willful Duke was not the best horse for a nervous rider.

"Well, we'll take him to the show tomorrow… if it's still okay with you to ride him?" She had asked, tears already forming in her eyes at the thought of having to part with the burly gray. "And then we'll make a decision on whether or not to keep him. He's just such a sweetie."

Cass had raised her eyebrows at that, glancing across at Charlie, who was biting her bottom lip to hold back an instinctive response.

"More spoiled than sweet, I think," Charlie had later remarked.

"Oh, I don't know," responded Cass, pursing her lips. "I think he has character."

"Well, you buy him, then," Charlie suggested. Cass laughed out loud. "You must be joking. I couldn't even afford to keep him in shoes."

A pale ray of early morning sunshine filtered through the drifting gray clouds, bringing the promise of another fine day, and Cass found herself suddenly looking forward to the show ahead. At least it would be a challenge and… who knew? Maybe Duke would surprise everyone.

The higgledy-piggledy arrangement of roofs that was Tall Trees came into view and she broke into a jog, wondering how they were managing without her at Hope Bank. What if Cosmic had already been sold; what if he was gone when she went over there next? A hollow emptiness welled up in her heart. It must be hard being a horse; even if you behaved yourself you could still be sold.

One day, she decided, she was going to have her own horse and she would keep it forever, no matter what.

The front gate of Tall Trees swung crookedly as Cass pushed it open, and the yard, she noted, had still not been swept. She looked around with a critical eye, wondering if she had time to do it before they set off.

"Cassie," cooed Mrs. A from over by a brand-new horse trailer.

Probably not, she answered her own question, heading across to where she and Anna were trying to load Duke. The gray cob had firmly planted his hooves in the earth and Cass had to smile at the expression on his face.

"Sorry I wasn't here yesterday," apologized Anna, her plump face pink with exertion.

"That's okay," smiled Cass, reaching out for the lead rope. Anna gave it up with a sigh of relief while Mrs. A beamed at her and patted Duke on his well-rounded rump. "Come along, darling," she begged.

Cass spun him around, getting close against his shoulder and looking forward, and then with a quick flick against his flank with the end of the rope she headed determinedly for the ramp. "Get up!" she roared, and the hefty gray dutifully plodded in to cries of delight from Mrs. A.

"Well done," she cried with glee, clapping her hands together.

"Shut the ramp, please," ordered Cass. "Before he decides to run back out again."

Just as Cass had hoped, Duke behaved like an angel in the practice ring. As soon as he was warmed up she headed for the practice fence, heart in mouth and heels pressed against his well-covered rib cage.

He approached the cross pole in a positive canter, heaving himself over with more enthusiasm than ability and landing with a heavy thud. Disappointment washed over her as she turned to approach the fence again, remembering something that Robert Ashton once said; "A good show jumping horse should leave the ground with a powerful thud and land in silence." Duke, it seemed, did it completely backwards.

She pushed him harder, increasing his pace. He launched himself as best he could, landing almost in a heap as his forefoot tipped the pole. Suddenly the clear round course they were about to attempt seemed nothing short of impossible.

"Well?" called Mrs. A, her bright eyes sparkling. "Do you think he'll get a clear?"

"I'll take a couple more practice jumps," responded Cass, side-stepping the question. Will he even get over the first fence was more to the point.

To be fair, the clumsy gray did his best, pricking his large ears and rising to the occasion. Cass chased him forward, encouraging him to use speed rather than having to depend solely on his somewhat limited ability. He stumbled over the first fence, met the second on an impossible stride but managed, somehow, to clear it, tipping the back pole with such a clatter that it almost brought him down. The pole bounced into the air and miraculously landed back down into its cups again. Cass dug in her heels; lady luck was on her side, so maybe anything was possible after all. As she trotted out of the ring in a cloud of steam, nine endless fences later, a surprised looking steward stepped forward to hand her a clear, round rosette. She took it with a beaming smile, relieved to be leaving the ring.

"We'll enter him in the open class next," announced a beaming Mrs. A.

"Look," Cass said, slipping to the ground as she patted Duke's damp neck, "I know he got a clear, but to be honest I don't really think that jumping is his thing. I'll come over and help Anna learn to ride him, though, and build up her confidence a bit. If you want me to, that is."

Mrs. A's carefully made-up face fell, but Anna beamed at her. "Will you... will you really help me?"

Cass shrugged. "Of course I will, and if it still doesn't work out then you'll just have to sell him."

"His jumping might improve," suggested Mrs. A tentatively, planting a kiss on Duke's broad forehead and leaving a perfectly shaped pair of ruby red lips

"I don't care if it doesn't," admitted Anna. "I hate jumping. All I really want is to be able to ride him out by myself."

"And you will," promised Cass rashly, hoping that she hadn't taken on too big a challenge.

It was just before they left for home that she first saw the elegant black Thoroughbred gelding.

He was staring into the distance, looking surprised, as if sensing an invisible foe, while his white-faced rider clung nervously to his neck strap; then suddenly he turned and looked straight at her. For Cass, for one fleeting moment, it felt as if she had been struck by lightning. Their connection was total, and all the bustle and noise of the busy showground faded into oblivion as she held the gaze of the beautiful black horse. He was the one; she knew it, as sure as if he had called her name. He was the horse who was to change her whole life. A shiver trickled down her spine, but was it to be in a good way or...?

Anna broke the spell.

"That's Tanya Bell and Typhoon," she announced. "He used to be stabled at Tall Trees, but Bob Marley, the boss, asked her to leave because Typhoon kept kicking his stable to pieces. He's a lunatic ex-racehorse, completely crazy, if you ask me."

From across the short distance the nervous gelding raised his noble head, snorting loudly as if the special moment between him and Cass had never been, his powerful muscles bunched to turn and flee. His terrified rider just seemed to freeze, gripping tightly on the reins and leaning forward over his arched crest.

Cass reacted without conscious thought, eager to help. "Kick him on," she yelled, hurrying toward them as he grabbed the reins from his rider's hands. "Just ride him forwards, around in a circle."

Her encouragement seemed to penetrate the girl's frozen state. She stared across at Cass with a helpless appeal in her wide pale eyes and then did the exact opposite of what she suggested, launching herself to the ground to land on wobbly legs, hanging desperately onto the buckle end of the reins while Typhoon spun around and around, fighting for his head.

"Look," Cass took a determined hold of the horse's rein, easily releasing it from the girl's only too willing hand. "You need to be a bit firmer with him, that's all, let him know who's boss."

"I think *he* is," groaned Tanya with a grateful smile.

"Definitely," echoed Anna, pleased to have found someone else as nervous as she.

Cass ignored them both, putting all her efforts into trying to control the panic-stricken horse.

"Steady, boy," she told him, taking a firm hold of the

reins and drawing herself up to her full height in order to get his attention, while not seeming to notice that her head hardly reached his withers. Typhoon snorted loudly and suddenly stopped his spinning, respecting her air of authority and sensing her lack of fear.

"Stand," she ordered. "Stand."

The elegant black horse looked down at her, his huge dark eyes once again connecting with the slightly built girl who had appeared so suddenly from nowhere.

Cass slid her hand up the side of his cheek to rub the back of his ear. "Easy, boy," she murmured and he lowered his head just for a moment, pressing his face fleetingly against her chest.

"You see..." she called. "He's nervous rather than just plain bad, and scared of his own shadow. If you take charge of him and let him see that *you're* not afraid then it will boost his confidence. Look..."

Typhoon dropped his head further, snuffling against Cass's hand. "You see? That's a sure sign that he's feeling calmer. The more nervous a horse is, the higher his head will go."

"Flight mode," added Anna knowingly.

"That's right," said Cass, nodding.

"But..." began Tanya nervously.

Her observation died, cut off by the arrival of a tall, sophisticated looking man wearing a stylish black coat. He strode determinedly toward them and stopped, glancing down at the gold watch on his left wrist.

"*What* is it?" he asked, glancing dismissively at Cassie before turning his attention to Tanya. "I thought I told you to be loaded and ready by three. I have an important meeting this evening, in case you've forgotten."

A pink hue colored Tanya's pale face, her eyes flickering

31

from side to side. "Sorry, Dad, I got kind of tied up. I'll go and load him now."

Flashing a grateful smile at Cass she reached for Typhoon's rein, hanging back to talk to her for a moment before turning away to fall in beside her tall, long-striding father. As the elegant black Thoroughbred skittered and pranced along beside them, Cass noted the rounded slump of the tall girl's shoulders with a shiver of alarm. Tanya was just so painfully nervous that there was no way she could ever manage the high-strung gelding by herself. He needed someone confident to help bolster his own courage. The moment when she first saw him filled her head, the moment when they had seemed to totally connect, and suddenly she knew... Typhoon needed her.

"And I thought *I* was scared," remarked Anna, bringing her back to the present. "Hey, are you okay? You look a little strange."

Cass smiled automatically, dragging her mind away from her crazy ideas. "Yes, of course, I'm fine. Would you like me to come over to Tall Trees soon and help *you* to ride Duke?"

Anna grinned. "That would be great. It's a pity that you can't help Tanya, though. I think she needs it even more than I do."

"I can't see her ever managing Typhoon," responded Cass. "He just seems so nervous and unpredictable."

"I think that there's something really weird about him," agreed Anna. "He's always staring into the shadows, as if he can see something that no one else can."

A shiver rippled down Cass's spine. "Don't say things like that," she pleaded. "She just asked me to ride him in the cross-country competition next weekend."

Anna stared at her in horror. "So that's what she was

talking to you about? And don't tell me that you actually agreed? Are you tired of living, or something?"

"He can't be that bad, can he?" Cass responded doubtfully.

Anna rolled her eyes. "Better you than me; he makes Duke look like a pussycat."

"Duke is a pussycat," giggled Cass. "And I'll prove it to you tomorrow. Come on, I can see your mother waving her arms at us from over by the trailer."

"Oh, no," groaned Anna. "I promised to be ready to go at three and it's almost quarter of four."

As the Anderson's four-wheel drive rolled gently across the grass toward the show entrance, Cass peered out the window, unable to get enough of the sights and sounds of her surroundings. One day, she promised herself, one day she would have her own horses, and then she'd show everyone. Maybe you'll show everyone next weekend, at the cross-country event, whispered an inner voice. Apprehension and excitement jostled for first place as she thought about riding the spirited Typhoon. Had they really connected, or was she just imagining it? And *were* their paths destined to cross? It had certainly felt that way at the time. Or maybe Anna was right and she was totally crazy to even try? Excitement flooded in, overpowering the prickle of nerves as she imagined him clearing fence after fence. Suddenly she couldn't wait.

CHAPTER 3

The yard at Hope Bank was already bustling with life when Cassie let herself in through the front gate. The snorting and snuffling sounds of hungry horses eager for breakfast filled the early morning air and a gentle steam rose from the far corner, where Silas was forking back the muckheap; everyone busily at work, organized and professional. After the chaos of Tall Trees it felt like coming home.

As she headed across the yard Cass found her gaze drawn at once to the large corner box that housed Cosmic. A gray head peered out, nervous and new.

"He went yesterday, I'm afraid," called out Mollie Ashton from over by the feed room. She had heard about Cass riding Cosmic and knew how disappointed she would be to find him gone. "He went to a lovely place though, if that's any consolation. I went with Robert to deliver him."

"If you had been here yesterday then you would have been able to say goodbye to him," admonished Laura. "Anyway, how did you do at the club show?"

Cass grimaced. "You really don't want to know; although, to be fair, we did get a rosette for a clear round."

"What?" Laura chortled, resting her fork against the stable wall. "On that great lump of a cob?"

"He's not really a lump," objected Cass, jumping to Duke's defense.

When she got close enough to see the laughter in Laura's warm brown eyes, however, her indignation faded. "Well… okay, maybe he is a little. He's never going to be a show jumper, that's for sure. Anyway, I promised to help Anna with him. To be honest, I felt sorry for her."

"Cassandra Truman," giggled Laura, shaking her head. "You really are totally hopeless. You feel sorry for everyone."

"Well, there's nothing wrong with caring about people," cut in Mollie, casting a disparaging smile in her daughter's direction. "And anyway, it's good to help people."

"Unfortunately," admitted Cass with a worried frown, "Anna isn't the only person I ended up offering to help – well, kind of help, anyway."

As Laura stepped toward her, eager to hear more, a bay horse ridden by Robert Ashton came clattering across the yard toward them, cutting the conversation short.

"The four block still needs to be mucked out when you three have finished chattering," he yelled, swinging down from the four-year-old stallion he had just been schooling. He threw the reins at Laura and she took them reluctantly, frowning up at him. "What's the matter with you this morning, Dad?"

Mollie's round face crinkled with concern as she stepped forward to take hold of her husband's arm. "What is it, hon?" she murmured.

Robert looked away, unsuccessfully disguising the emotion that ravaged his features. "Scott Ridley just called me on my cell… Cosmic twisted his gut last night and they had to put him down."

"No!"

Mollie's cry of objection echoed around and around inside Cassie's head. How could such a beautiful, spirited gelding possibly be dead when he was so very much alive just two days ago? All that life and energy and promise… It was so unfair.

Her head was still spinning with the injustice of it as she helped untack the sweet-natured young stallion, Forester.

"It happens, unfortunately," sighed Laura, unbuckling the throatlatch and sliding the bridle headpiece forward over his ears. He lowered his head, willingly releasing the gleaming snaffle bit. "Dad's best show jumper died of a twisted gut when I was five; I think that's what stopped him from competing more seriously." Laura's attractive features clouded with the memory. "He was totally devastated. I'll never forget it."

"And what about the money?" asked Cass, suddenly realizing the repercussions. "Scott Ridley must have paid a fortune for Cosmic. Will he want his money back?"

"Who knows," remarked Laura, shrugging. "Poor old Dad, all that work and effort wasted."

"All that life wasted," echoed Cass, brushing away a sudden rush of tears.

The shock of Cosmic's death left a shadow that settled like a black cloud over the normally cheerful yard at Hope Bank. "These things happen," was Silas's calm observation when Robert finally reappeared later that morning.

"It doesn't make it any easier though, does it?" responded Robert. "Scott had him insured, thank goodness, but no amount of money can replace a horse like that."

In the face of such gloom Cass even forgot about her promise to ride Typhoon until Laura reminded her of the conversation that had been so suddenly interrupted earlier that morning.

"By the way, you didn't tell me who else you had promised to help," she remarked while carefully measuring scoops for the late afternoon feeds.

Cassie crouched down as each bucket was filled, happily plunging her hands into the fragrant, sticky mixture and stirring vigorously.

"There's a mixing stick over there," advised Laura.

Cass shook her head. "You can't do a decent job with that, and anyway I like doing it by hand."

Laura put the scoop back into the feed bin and wiped her hands on her jodhpurs. "You haven't answered my question yet," she remarked.

Cass looked up, meeting her inquiring gaze with a ready smile. "Oh, just a girl from the show. She has a black Thoroughbred that I agreed to take around the cross-country course next weekend." She stood, rubbing her aching thighs. "Hey, why don't you take Steel? You said he needed a wider experience."

"This horse…" Laura narrowed her eyes, ignoring her suggestion. "… Is he a bit difficult?"

Cass laughed. "Well, I haven't ridden him yet, but from what I've seen of him – and that's not much – he's definitely very nervous."

"What's his owner's name?"

The serious expression in Laura's eyes sent an involuntary shudder down Cass's spine. "Tanya something," she replied cautiously. "Tanya… Bell, that's it, Tanya Bell."

"Call and tell her that you can't do it."

Cass laughed out loud. "I can't do that, I've promised. And anyway, Typhoon can't be that bad; I mean, well, she was riding him at the show yesterday."

"In the equitation class, I'll bet," cried Laura. "She wouldn't dare take him over a fence. The horse is a raving lunatic."

"He's just nervous," insisted Cass, annoyed at her friend's intervention and, secretly, a bit more concerned than she was letting on.

"I mean it, Cass." Laura took hold of her arm. "Make up an excuse."

37

"It's alright for you," objected Cass, shrugging her hand off. "With your lovely youngster and all your opportunities. I have to take any ride I can get, and I'm not going to let you scare me off this one. At least someone asked me to ride a quality horse, for once."

Suddenly Laura was giggling. "When have you ever been scared of riding anything?" she chortled. "Quality or not. Anyway, it's often the cob types that are more awkward."

"Exactly," agreed Cass, thinking of Duke. "So please don't spoil it for me... after all, surely the worst I can do is fall off."

"I'm not trying to spoil it for you," blurted out Laura. "I'm concerned, that's all. Anyway, let's just hope that I don't get to say I told you so. Come on; let's dole these feeds out. Dad has gone to turn the new gray out into riverside meadow, and knowing him he'll probably let Bobby come back with him."

"That's all we need," groaned Cass, picking up two buckets. "And hey..."

She caught Laura's eye, grinning awkwardly. "I'm sorry for picking on you, and I'm not really jealous... honestly."

"Let's just forget it," suggested Laura. "Be careful, that's all I'm saying."

The warm glow of late afternoon sunshine cast a golden light across the neatly swept yard as the two girls stepped out of the feed room. A dozen horses nickered loudly, eager for their feeds, tossing their heads over their stable doors and Tom, the black and white stable cat, rubbed affectionately across their legs. Cassie paused for a moment to talk to him, just as another sound filtered into her consciousness, a high-pitched whinny closely followed by the thud of unshod hooves.

38

"Here comes Bobby," shrieked Laura, heading off across the yard just as the tubby little chestnut appeared, cantering toward them from around the back of the barn with Robert Ashton following behind. Before Laura had even managed to reach the first stable he was already trying to plunge his head into one of her buckets, and with one huge lurch he managed to dislodge it from her grip, spilling its contents across the ground.

"I'll get a head collar," offered Robert, grinning sheepishly. "Poor little guy just wanted some company."

"Some food is more like it," laughed Laura, shaking her head. "Honestly, Dad, you are impossible. You just seem to have a blind spot when it comes to this little horror."

"We go back a long way, don't we, boy?" he responded, scratching the little pony's withers.

From across the yard Cass watched, a lump of sadness choking her throat. How unjust was nature, she thought, to let a young horse like Cosmic, with a brilliant future ahead of him, die so tragically when old Bobby seemed set to go on forever.

"That's life, missy," observed Silas, clamping his gnarled hand down onto her shoulder. "You just have to get on with it."

Cass thought about Silas's wise words a couple of days later while cycling down the street toward Brewster's farm, where Typhoon was stabled. *You just have to get on with it.* It was good advice, she decided, advice that she was determined to follow, starting today. No matter how difficult it was going to be she would just get on with it, and it was sure to be worth the effort, for the moment that she first saw the beautiful black Thoroughbred still lingered in the forefront of her mind. They had connected in some special, awesome way; there was no doubt in her mind about that. Somehow Typhoon was meant to figure in her life, and today she was going to find out how.

The farm came into view at last, a square white house, low stone buildings and an old-fashioned cobblestoned drive. She jumped off her bike, leaned it carefully against the wall and headed anxiously across to where she could see Tanya's dad striding impatiently up and down beside their silver four-wheel drive and matching trailer.

"Sorry," she called. "Am I late?"

Tanya rolled her eyes. "Dad has a meeting and he has to drop us off early, so we're already loaded up and ready to roll. I tried to call you, but there was no answer."

"Sorry," repeated Cass, disappointment flooding over her at not being able to see Typhoon again before they set off. "I'm afraid I left my phone at home."

Paul Bell gave a relieved snort, already climbing into the driver's seat. "Come on," he grumbled. "You're here now, so let's get going."

As soon as they were out of the entrance he put his foot down hard on the throttle, driving fast along the narrow lane. Too fast, thought Cass, as he swung the big vehicle around a hairpin bend, bringing a thud from the trailer behind. No wonder poor Typhoon was a bag of nerves; it's a wonder he loaded at all. She glanced at Tanya, who pulled an apologetic face. "He has to be at the office by eight thirty," she explained nervously.

Cass just looked out of the window, biting her bottom lip; as far as she was concerned, there was no excuse for driving so fast when you had a horse on board, and if he didn't slow down soon she would have to say something.

"Look, there it is," cried a relieved Tanya. Cass exhaled, unclenching her fists. Just up ahead she could see a stream of horse trailers pouring through a field gate and further away, across the hillside and on into the woods beyond, were dotted various scary looking cross-country jumps. Nerves jangled inside her, taking her breath away. If only she had had a chance to go and actually have a ride on Typhoon before the competition she would have felt better, but it just hadn't seemed to happen. It didn't matter, she decided, remembering her decision. *"You just have to get on with it."*

"This is it!" exclaimed Tanya as her father pulled into a narrow gap between two imposing-looking horse trailers.

"For better or worse," groaned Cass.

Tanya flashed her a worried glance. "You haven't changed your mind, have you?"

She shook her head determinedly. "Course not. I'm looking forward to it."

"Okay, girls," announced Paul Bell, cutting the engine. "That's my secretary's car over there; she's picking me up. I'll be back around four."

"See you, Dad," responded Tanya. "Wish us luck," she added, but he was already striding off toward a sleek black car whose glamorous blonde driver was waving eagerly.

"Come on," urged Cassie, sensing Tanya's disappointment in her father's lack of interest and eager to get her attention. "Let's get him unloaded."

"You'd better walk the course first," Tanya suggested, her mind clicking back into the present. "I'll stay here and get him ready."

Cass hesitated, desperate to see Typhoon and yet also strangely apprehensive. "Well... if you're sure."

Suddenly Tanya smiled. "Of course I'm sure. I'm just glad that you're riding him and not me, and anyway I should be used to my dad being so busy by now."

The course, while daunting, was definitely very jumpable, thought Cass as she walked down the back of the hill and headed for the woods. There were plenty of options if she decided that Typhoon didn't feel capable of taking on the bigger fences. Relief descended, settling her jangling nerves. After all, maybe he would soar over them all.

As she jogged back to the trailer half an hour or so later, she could see Tanya still sitting on the ramp, her arms wrapped around her knees. "I thought that you were unloading him?" she called. "There isn't much time, and I haven't even sat on him yet."

"He just looks so stressed," explained Tanya, a flush spreading across her pale cheeks. "I thought he might take off on me."

"Well, how did you manage last time?"

"He took off on me," grinned Tanya.

Suddenly Cass was grinning back. "Come on, then. You get his tack and I'll get him out."

Cassie's first impression as she slid into the saddle and took up the reins was that Typhoon was totally wired, as tense as a coiled spring. His ears were everywhere, flicking back and forth, and he tossed his beautiful head constantly.

She rode him forward, marveling at his generous stride. Never had she sat upon anything with such power – except for poor Cosmic, of course, but he was a whole different ball game. This horse was like a bouncy ball. Suddenly she felt as if they could take on the world. "Come on, then," she cried with glee. "Let's get over to the practice fence."

He tried to bolt twice on their way across the showground, filled with fear by every tiny unexpected movement, as if aware of something that his rider couldn't see. Cass sat firm, ready with a half halt and a firmly spoken word, and he seemed to calm down, taking confidence from her determined authority. Half a dozen circuits of the practice area and she led him to a small cross pole, feeling his surge of power with elation. Now, this horse really did leave the ground with a thud and land in silence.

"He feels great," she called across to where Tanya watched in awe.

"Don't underestimate him," Tanya warned just as the big black horse clamped down his tail, staring into the distance. Head way up above the bridle, he took off toward the trees, the bit firmly clenched between his teeth. Cass scrambled with the reins, taken by surprise, gathering them awkwardly before setting one hand on his neck and sitting back to take a pull. He leaped through the air, defying her efforts, and she threw herself forward to grab the bit ring, hauling him hard around in a circle. He suddenly stopped dead, totally deflated, head down and sides heaving and Cass felt a tremor of fear. There was something much more to this horse than either just plain awkwardness or fear; it was as if he had a hidden agenda.

"I told you to watch out," called a relieved Tanya, running toward them.

Cass could hear her own heartbeat thudding in her ears and the palms of her hands felt clammy; this made Duke's clumsy and awkward halfhearted protests seem like a joke. "I'd better keep my wits about me," she smiled determinedly, ignoring the negative vibes that threatened to swamp her.

"I think it's almost your turn to start," exclaimed Tanya. "If you're still sure that you want to, that is…"

43

Cass grinned, taking a breath. "Of course I want to."

The first fence came easily, an extended stride within the rhythm of the powerful horse's canter. Cass felt her nerves disintegrate, replaced by a burst of elation.

"Come on, boy," she murmured, reaching forward to run her hand down the firm muscles of his neck as they turned down hill toward a log pile. Typhoon pricked his ears, clearing it by a foot, and they thundered on toward a wall. Cass steadied him, aware of the drop on the other side, but he leaped it with glee. She concentrated on breathing, blinking away the tears brought on by the rush of the wind in her face. Where now? The wood loomed ahead, dark and mysterious.

As they entered the wooded area she first sensed her mount's change of mood. His almost electric tension tingled beneath her, increasing her heart rate.

"Steady, boy," she cautioned, trying to get his attention, but he seemed oblivious to her commands, as if his mind was elsewhere. She kicked him firmly, taking a half halt, and felt him come back on track as they headed for a set of gates across the path. A surge of easy power, two strides, another effort and they were galloping through the trees, alone in the eerie silence of the wood. Cass clung to the moment, savoring the sound of echoing hooves on the firm pathway and absorbing the elation that made her heart sing. This was what real riding was all about...

When they turned to leave the woodland for the wide sweep of open grassland she felt Typhoon falter. His head went up sharply, ears pinned back against his skull as he suddenly veered off to the right. Cass fought to control him, legs clamped on, heaving on the reins, desperately trying to get him back on course and to listen to her futile commands...

She knew that she had lost him the moment he took a

huge leap into the undergrowth, tearing the reins from her fingers. After that she was just clinging on in desperation as he swerved between the trees, totally oblivious to the rider on his back, crashing her legs against solid trunks as the branches tore at her face and arms. Fear descended in a mind-blowing cloud, swamping everything. She had to stop him… With one last desperate attempt she regained her balance, fighting for control and suddenly, unbelievably, Typhoon was sliding on his forehand, his front hooves digging into the dirt.

As the powerful horse beneath her skidded to a halt Cass felt a warm rush of elation flood her whole body, closely followed by a strange lethargy. Her reins fell loose on Typhoon's warm damp neck as she collapsed across it; the aroma of horse and sweat filled her nostrils. She didn't foresee his next reaction, didn't anticipate the awesome surge as the muscles of his hindquarters bunched beneath him.

He sank down on his hocks and Cass scrambled for the reins, but it was too late, and suddenly he was rising up in a mighty rear, his shoulders lifting before her as she threw herself forward, grabbing his mane as his head came back.

His skull hit hers with a crack that took away all sense of reality, apart from the ringing, awesome pain that consumed her whole being. She was lost in another place, where dreams and reality fused together lopsidedly and a strange electric tingle seared her soul… Typhoon just moved on, ears pricked now, carrying his half conscious rider toward a distant crackling sound.

CHAPTER 4

Typhoon came to a halt at last, sidling nervously and champing on the bit while Cass collapsed against his neck, trying to control the erratic thudding of her heart by taking large deep breaths. Her head ached unbearably, as if someone inside her skull was wielding a hammer, and her limbs seemed unable to carry out the garbled commands of her brain.

Where was she, and where was the cross-country course? She shook her head, trying to shake the weird crackling that kept her from thinking clearly, blinking hard to focus on the blurrily distorted images that slid in and out of her vision. Ahead of her she could see a light; softly fuzzy as if shining through a mist. Its comforting radiance seemed to call to her from across her weirdly flickering surroundings and she took up the reins with numb fingers, urging Typhoon toward it while trying to remember… what? They had been galloping, she knew that, pounding across the countryside taking the fences in their stride. Memories slid back into her consciousness, her memories comfortingly familiar: the power of movement beneath her, Typhoon's mighty leap, and their awesome, brief period of total connection.

She had managed to regain control when he bolted with her, she remembered that clearly… but then what? Everything after was blurry and indistinct. She decided that she had to find the cross-country course again and looked hopelessly around for a familiar landmark while desperately trying to stay calm. When had it started to get dark, and where was Tanya? Surely she would come looking for her soon.

The sound of hooves clip-clopped steadily along the tarmac of a narrow country road, echoing in rhythm with the thumping of her head. Well, they were on a road, at least, so it must go somewhere; hope flared inside her, soothing the jittery nerves that danced beneath her rib cage.

The hooves became louder, mismatched, losing the rhythm. There was another horse… another horse approaching at a trot. If there was a horse then it must have a rider, so at least she could ask where she was.

They appeared from the weirdly fizzing mist, distant and indistinct, like characters on a faltering TV screen, a silvery gray horse and its shadowy rider, moving in and out of her vision. Had the whole world gone totally out of focus? Cass tried to smile but her face felt wooden and stiff, as if it belonged to someone else.

The rider moved his mouth but no words came out… Or was it just that she couldn't hear him speaking because of the strange high-pitched crackling sound that vibrated through the air? Was he even real at all? Suddenly he looked *very* real: young, late teens and ruggedly handsome, with clear blue eyes.

"Excuse me, can you tell me where we are?"

Cassie's voice sounded too loud in her ears, as if it was trapped inside her head. Was that how he felt too? She tried again. "Hello… hello…"

He seemed to smile in her direction but their eyes slid past each other, not connecting, his image wavering in and out of view as his mouth began silently moving again, opening and closing like a bizarre human fish.

"I can't hear you."

She leaned toward him, tangling her fingers in Typhoon's mane, disappointment a heavy ache inside her chest as

she called out again and again while he just stared straight through her, distant and aloof. Could he see her at all?

Slowly the image of horse and rider began to flicker and fade, distorted and unreal. Cass called out once more, totally oblivious to everything but her desperation for them to stay. "Don't go…"

Rain splashed unexpectedly down onto the road ahead, heavy droplets dancing on the paved surface and stinging her face as a wind came up from nowhere and turned them into slanting daggers. Typhoon spun around, turning his tail to the sudden onslaught of weather and Cass fought to control him, gulping back her tears. It was almost dark, she didn't know where she was, and her whole world seemed to have been turned totally upside down. Taking a deep breath, she tried to stay focused, unclenching her hands and urging her reluctant mount forwards again. She had to go on, there was nothing else to do. Typhoon tossed his head in protest and she turned her face into the rain, clinging frantically to some semblance of sanity. Had he really been here at all, the young man on the silver gray horse? She saw his face in her mind's eye, too clear to be a dream… Maybe he was just another part of the nightmare she was in. Maybe there had never been a cross-country competition at all and she would wake at any moment, at home in her own bed. It was a comforting thought.

Beneath her Typhoon sidled, solid and real, belying the idea. She squeezed him on and, suddenly obedient, he broke eagerly into a jog-trot, prancing sideways along the road. The sudden lurching movement brought with it a wave of dizziness, forcing her to cling helplessly onto the saddle, struggling to ease back on the reins again. To her relief he slowed his pace at once, raising his head, ears sharply pricked toward the skyline.

49

Cass followed his gaze toward a solid black mass of hills that stood out against the pale gray of the sky, looming and ominous. A shiver rippled down her spine, consuming her, and her teeth chattered painfully as she tried to focus. Was she going to die here, all alone in this strange place?

The light that filtered unexpectedly into her strange gray world took her by surprise, bringing with it a ray of hope as an iridescent moon slipped slowly from behind the dark clouds. It edged the hedgerows in silver, casting its pale beam across the wet gray tarmac as the driving rain magically cleared, shining on something in the grass on the shoulder of the road. A sign! Could it really be a sign?

She rode toward it eagerly, trying to read the words inscribed in black; at least now she would know where she was. HAWK RIDGE, it read. She repeated the name out loud. A real place with a real name... but where on earth was Hawk Ridge, and which way was home?

She would just have to try to go back the way she had come, she decided, turning Typhoon around and heading him down the road. Surely she would find someone she could ask soon...

She saw the horse and rider again as she rounded the next corner, trotting briskly by intently, and totally oblivious to her and Typhoon. Their images flickered slightly, clear to the eye and yet somehow insubstantial, making her feel like an outside observer. With a sense of helplessness, she reached out her hand. "Please... do you know where we are?"

The sudden blast of an angry horn drowned her voice, ricocheting around inside her head. The silver horse stopped in its tracks, trying to spin around as the horn sounded again, heralding the approach of the huge truck that loomed way up above the hedgerow, appearing from nowhere, the driver's face a vacant white blur in the high window.

For one brief moment the mighty vehicle towered ominously above them, a flash of red and silver, and in a breath it was gone, just as if it had never been there at all ... But the damage was already done.

The other horse reared bolt upright, struggling to gain balance. Its rider threw himself forwards, iron shod hooves slammed back down onto the road again and the horse leaped into gallop, a silver blur of power slipping and sliding along the pavement. The young man's face was a stark white mask as he fought with the reins, his eyes two gaping dark holes as he finally lost control... His mount plunged, veering sharply to the left, and then they were gone, crashing over and over, down the steep bank beside the road.

When Cass dared to look again, peering down the steep incline, the horse was standing on three legs, head down and foreleg swinging hopelessly... and its rider? The young man lay as still as death, his body twisted at an impossible angle, and she knew, deep down in her gut she knew... he wasn't breathing... Her whole body froze... she had to get help.

Their images wavered, insubstantial and transparent. She shook her head to clear it and suddenly they were gone, disappearing into the crackling fizzy blur, like the truck that caused the tragedy in the first place. Still, she couldn't leave like this; she had to do something, to tell someone.

She headed Typhoon back along the grassy shoulder, kicking him into a gallop, but then he balked, rearing up and swinging around to avoid... what? There was something in their way. What was it, and when had the shoulder become so smooth, green and well tended? She tried to turn away, to push him past the obstacle, but it loomed before her, forcing her attention. Typhoon snorted, blowing hard through his nostrils. Why... it was a headstone, a marble headstone, shiny and new. A cold hand clutched at her heart as her eyes devoured the inscription that loomed out at her...

In loving memory of
MICHAEL MILLER
February 5th, 1993 - August 30th, 2010

It was 2010, now... but it was still only June. The truth dawned on her: this person, whoever he may be, wasn't even dead yet!

Suddenly Cass knew what she must do; somehow, for some reason, she had been given a glimpse of the future and now she had to try and find this Michael Miller and change his fate before it was too late. For surely he had to have been the young man who was riding the silver gray horse... the young man who had plunged down the steep bank to...

Shaking her head to banish the images, she gathered up Typhoon's reins, kicking him on. The marble headstone was gone now and the lane stretched out before her, lighter somehow and far less daunting. Way up ahead she could see a clump of trees, and was that a horse and rider? Eagerly she pushed into a trot, heading toward them and trying to ignore the violent banging inside her skull.

"Just lie still, dear... that's it. You had a nasty fall."

Kind hands, stroking her face.

"Don't try to move."

Everything was jumbled and blurry, the pale face above her vague and shapeless.

"Let me through…"

A deeper voice boomed out inside her aching head.

"You'll be fine now, dear. We're going to take you to the hospital."

"No!"

Her whole being rose up in objection. There was something she had to do, something important… but what?

Kind hands holding her down, lifting her, a stinging sensation in her arm; the pain inside her head rose higher and higher, settling into a point way up at the top of her skull. Then slowly it totally evaporated, leaving behind a languid detachment that settled over her in a comforting blanket.

Cass opened her eyes to see a light; bright and white and alien. She struggled to sit up. Where was she?

"You're all right now, love, don't worry."

Her grandmother's voice, soft in her ears, comforting; a warm hand on her arm.

"You had a fall, but you're going to be fine. Just a bit of a concussion."

When she opened her eyes again Granddad Bill was looking down at her, concern in his eyes. "You're a naive girl, taking a chance like that."

Chances… chances? She remembered Typhoon. Where was he?

"Typhoon?"

The word came out in a croak.

"If you mean that lunatic horse you tried to ride, then he's fine," snorted her grandmother, "although I don't know why you're concerned, after what he's done to you."

Suddenly everything cleared, settling into place. The cross-country, the elation of clearing the jumps, her fear as Typhoon galloped out of control… and the young man on the silver horse. Something inside clamped tight shut… *MICHAEL MILLER*…

She tried to sit up. "I have to save him!"

Her grandparents exchanged a worried glance. "Save who, love?" asked her grandmother.

"I saw an accident… in the street… I have to warn Michael."

"No, Cass." Granddad Bill's eyes were troubled, gazing down at her. "You had a fall, that's all. It's just a concussion, and whatever you think you saw must just be a dream you had, you know, when you hit your head."

Cass reached a hand to her face, remembering how Typhoon's head had crashed into it as he reared. It hurt beneath her touch. "But I didn't fall…"

"You probably don't remember, that's all," reassured her grandmother. "They're funny things, concussions."

Cass turned her face away from them, trying to sort out the turmoil inside her brain. Had it all really been just a dream? The memory of the young man's face slid into her consciousness, the image of his twisted body lying at the bottom of the bank…and the silver horse, its foreleg swinging uselessly. She choked back a cry, trying to focus.

"She seems a little confused," broke in another voice. "We were going to let her go home after lunch, but maybe she'd better stay in for another night."

"No." Cass looked up into the face of the white-coated doctor. "No, honestly, I'm not at all confused now. I feel absolutely fine."

He smiled back pleasantly. "Well, we'll see how you are after lunch."

Cass sat in the back of Granddad Bill's ancient car, huddled up, arms around her knees, trying to ignore the pain that still thudded inside her head. She couldn't get the image of the young man on the gray horse from her mind. Was his name really Michael Miller, and was it his tombstone she saw? Or, as her grandparents insisted, had it all been just a crazy concussed dream? She shivered, pulling the blanket more closely around her. Would she ever really know?

The dates loomed back into her consciousness, February 5th, 1993 - August 30th, 2010. That would make him just seventeen when he died... whoever he was.

"Have you ever heard of a place called Hawk Ridge?"

Her voice sounded croaky, as if it belonged to someone else.

"Hawk Ridge?" Her grandfather frowned, glancing back from the driver's seat. "It rings a bit of a bell, but I don't know where it is."

"It sounds more like a name from a cowboy film, if you ask me," added her grandmother. "Why do you want to know, anyway?"

Cass shrugged. "Doesn't matter, it just came into my head, that's all."

"Nothing to do with that crazy dream you keep going on about, does it? You know what the doctor said. Any problems and we're going to take you straight back to the hospital."

"I'm fine, Gran, honestly. Can we visit the Brewster's farm to make sure that Typhoon is alright?"

"Definitely not," cut in Granddad Bill. "It's home and bed for you, young lady, and if that friend of yours has any sense at all she'll be putting the crazy animal up for sale right away."

Cass thought about the big black Thoroughbred, remembering the brief moments when they had totally jelled, taking

55

the fences in his stride, his ears sharply pricked before her. "He's incredibly talented," she responded. "But just a little high-strung."

"Well, make sure that you never ride him again," insisted her grandmother.

Cass just turned her face away to gaze from the window without responding, suddenly longing to feel his awesome stride beneath her again. He needed understanding, that's all, she was sure of it.

The images of the young man and his horse were still in her mind two days later, when her grandmother finally allowed her to go back to Hope Bank, with strict instructions that she was not to ride for another few days. She walked into the neat and tidy yard, breathing in the aroma of horse with a sense of homecoming.

"Told you so," called Laura, appearing from the barn with a hay net slung over either shoulder.

Cass laughed, ignoring the thudding pain that still lingered inside her head. "The part just before the accident was well worth it, though."

Laura flicked back the curtain of shiny dark hair that had fallen across her face, dumped her hay nets on the ground and fumbled in her pocket for a band to tie it back. "Cassandra Truman, you are completely crazy," she exclaimed. "He bolted with you, didn't he, and you fell off?"

Cass frowned, remembering. "No... he did bolt with me, that's true, but then he reared up and hit me in the face..."

"So you didn't actually fall off?"

"They say that I did, but I can't remember... in fact..."

Laura looked at her eagerly. "In fact what?"

"Nothing..." Cass had been looking forward to telling

Laura about the boy and his horse, but suddenly it all seemed a little ridiculous. Maybe her grandparents were right after all... maybe it had been just a very real dream. "Have you ever heard of a place called Hawk Ridge?" she asked tentatively.

Laura shook her head. "It sounds like a place from a cowboy movie," she smiled.

"That's exactly what Gran said," sighed Cass. "Here, give me one of those hay nets. Have you finished all the mucking out?"

Suddenly she wanted to work until every muscle ached with effort, and she was too tired to even think of Michael Miller and his silver horse, plunging to their doom. There, she had admitted it to herself; she really did believe that the young man in her dream was the Michael Miller on the tombstone. But then again, hadn't she just thought of the whole experience as a dream? Maybe her grandparents were right after all, and that really was it... just a stupid, meaningless dream.

"Are you alright, Cass?"

Laura's concerned voice brought Cass sharply back from her reverie. "Yes, of course I am. Just tell me what needs to be done and I'll get to work."

She picked up a hay net and set off across the yard. August 30th, 2010, two and a half months away... But even if it was some kind of weird premonition and she actually found this Michael Miller, she would never get him to believe her anyway.

"I think you'd better stick to just brushing horses," suggested Laura, staring at her curiously. "Unless you want to go back home. You look awful."

Cass determinedly pushed all her crazy fantasies to the very back of her mind as she swung the net up onto her shoulder. "Thanks for the compliment," she smiled. "But don't worry about me. Honestly, I really am fine."

That was it, she decided, she was going to take her grandparents' advice and forget her stupid dream. "I'll just hand this net out and then you can tell me who needs to be groomed."

CHAPTER 5

Cass stood back to look over her handiwork, her muscles aching deliciously with the efforts of the last half an hour. Aching was good, she decided; it brought her sharply and clearly into the practical world of the stable yard and made her forget all the crazy memories that still crept in when least expected.

It had been over a week now since the misadventure and she had mostly managed to put the experience behind her – except in the dead of night, of course. She hadn't yet plucked up the courage to go and see Typhoon either, still needing time to try and distance herself from the events that haunted her dreams… maybe tomorrow.

She shivered, reaching out her fork to pat down a final wayward piece of straw. There, the bed was neatly laid – golden banks, perfectly ready for the new horse that would be arriving later that afternoon. With a final glance at her handiwork Cass closed the stable door behind her and went out into the early summer sunshine. She hadn't even helped Duke yet, she realized, guiltily remembering her promise.

Taking in her surroundings with new eyes she found herself comparing them, favorably, to Tall Trees while wondering how Anna was making out with the chunky gray cob. Maybe she should go there this afternoon.

She glanced at her watch. Laura had just disappeared into town with her mother, Silas had gone off with Robert to deliver a horse and Jack Donelly had called in sick… again. She had finished all the stables anyway, and she really didn't feel like being on her own at the moment, so maybe she should go and see how Anna was doing this afternoon. *And what about Typhoon?* The whispered words inside her head made her heart beat faster.

Refusing to worry about the black Thoroughbred gelding and the young man she had nicknamed M, she set off on her bike, along the road toward Tall Trees. It would be nice to see Duke again, she decided. His problems seemed so small compared with Typhoon's, and she really would like to see Anna gain confidence with him. And tomorrow... Her heart rate increased again. Tomorrow maybe she *would* go to Brewster's farm to see Tanya and Typhoon, for despite her horrific experience with him, she couldn't help thinking that there must be a way to calm the spirited gelding down. He was so talented; if she truly won his trust then they could achieve unimaginable heights. But what if Tanya now wanted to sell him off cheap? Her heart sank. No matter how cheap he was, there was no way that she would ever be able to afford him, and even if her grandparents had the money to buy him for her they never would, not after the way he behaved on the cross-country course.

The jumble of buildings that made up Tall Trees came into view just then, taking her attention. The yard was still not swept, she noted, and the muckheap was sprawled out across the yard in an untidy mess. A bay horse appeared, ridden by a smiling middle-aged woman wearing pink jodhpurs. Its coat was shining and it tossed its head eagerly, looking bright-eyed and happy, just like its rider. Oh well, decided Cass, I don't suppose the horses mind how untidy the place is as long as they're well cared for. That's what really matters.

❀ ❀ ❀ ❀ ❀

Duke was in his stable, chomping happily on his hay net, ears drooping and eyes half closed.

"She hasn't ridden him since you took him to the show, you know," remarked Charlie, suddenly appearing from the box next door.

Cass sighed. "That's too bad, he needs the work and he's not really that bad. Just a little unruly."

Charlie nodded, shaking her blonde ponytail. "I agree; he just doesn't *get* the work, that's the trouble. Mrs. A asked me if I would exercise him for them, but I just haven't had the time. Maybe you could ride him today?"

Cass hesitated for a moment before replying. "No, I don't think so. To be honest, I haven't seen Anna for a while."

Charlie picked up two empty feed buckets and headed off across the yard. "Well, I'm sure they wouldn't mind. I think Mrs. A is around somewhere, if you want to ask her."

Cass grabbed a yard brush; suddenly she needed to do something simple to calm her thoughts down. Her head was all over the place. "I'll sweep up, if you like," she called to Charlie's retreating figure. The slight blonde girl turned to look back at her, a beaming smile lighting up her heart shaped face. "That would be great, thanks. As you can see, I don't have much time for cleaning. It's not that I don't like to see the place looking nice; I just have to put the horse's care first, and there never seems to be time for anything else."

It took almost an hour for Cass to get the stable yard reasonably organized. One of the boarding stable horse owners, a small, dark-haired woman named Hilda, tentatively offered to give her a hand, and they started on the ominous muckheap with fervor. By the time Mrs. A finally arrived with Anna in tow, Cass and Hilda were perched on the wall sipping tea, provided by a grateful Charlie.

"Maybe we should start rotating?" suggested Hilda. "You know, take turns cleaning the place. It looks so much better."

"And make it a part of the boarding stable contract," added Cass. "Everyone has to fork back the muck heap and sweep around their own area."

Mrs. A made a face, but Charlie nodded eagerly. "Definitely, I'll have a word with Mr. Marley. He used to do it himself, but his arthritis is too bad now."

"I don't mind," Anna butted in, smiling. "I think it's much better to see everything looking so neat."

"So, are we going to see Duke now?" asked Mrs. A impatiently, already setting off across the neatly swept yard.

Raising her hand to Hilda, Cass stood up. "Thanks for your help."

"Thanks for yours," she responded with a warm smile.

"Ditto," agreed Charlie. "I'm tired of trying to do everything myself."

It was strange, thought Cass, riding the chunky gray around the outdoor ring, to think that she had ever imagined Duke was difficult. After riding Typhoon she didn't think that she would ever find any horse difficult again.

"He just needs to know who's boss," she called across to Anna, who was standing by the gate hopping eagerly from foot to foot.

"But will he behave for me?" she responded.

"Let's find out," suggested Cass. "Come on, I'll help you."

Half an hour later a delighted Anna was trotting happily around the outdoor ring, watched by a beaming Mrs. A. Duke had misbehaved once or twice but, inspired by

Cass, Anna had sat tight, kept her contact and ridden him strongly forward. Surprised at his rider's newfound authority and too lazy to object, it seemed that the gray cob had decided to behave himself at last.

"See," called Cass. "You can do it. Always be ready, though. You know, keep your legs on and don't drop the contact. Next time I come we'll take him out along the road, if you like."

Anna's expression said it all. "When, though?" she cried. "When will you come again?"

Cass shrugged. "Well, it's the school vacation next week, so just give me a buzz and I'll come over one afternoon after I've been to Hope Bank."

Cycling slowly homewards along the road, Cass felt a glow of satisfaction that brought a new surge of self-confidence. Helping Anna made her feel surer of herself somehow, and she was well aware that since the Typhoon incident she had lost some of the determined drive that had always overridden any nerves. The truth was, she'd failed to re-seat the big black Thoroughbred; she was well aware of that. For the first time ever, she'd been unable to re-mount after a fall. Casting her thoughts back to the moment when it all went so horribly wrong, she still couldn't really believe that she'd fallen off at all.

Suddenly she was filled with a strong desire to ride Typhoon again, to get the feeling he had given her as they took those first few fences. It had been awesome, and a talent like that had to be worth pursuing. But then again…

An image of the young man on the gray horse sprang into her mind. That mind-blowing dream couldn't have been real, though, could it?

She decided that tomorrow she would go to Brewster's

farm. If Tanya was there then maybe she would even ride Typhoon, and if not… if not then she would just spend some time with him, try to get inside his head and feel once again that spark of connection that had bound her to him since the moment they first saw each other across the bustling show ground.

With a new sense of purpose and prickling excitement dancing inside her chest she increased her pace, her legs furiously pumping the pedals as her dreams flooded back.

To Cass's disappointment, she awoke the next morning to rain battering against her window. By the time she was ready to set off for Hope Bank it had settled to a gray, incessant drizzle, and a heavy cloud of mist blanked out the world.

"You can't go out in this!" cried her grandmother. "Why don't you stay home for a while, and see if it clears up?"

Cass remained undeterred. "A little rain won't hurt," she insisted.

"Then make sure that you wear something waterproof, and don't be home too late."

"I won't," smiled Cass, already fumbling in the closet for a jacket.

Ten minutes later, standing up on her bike pedals, her jodhpur-clad legs working like pistons, she felt grateful for the bright blue hooded waterproof jacket her grandmother had insisted she wear. At least she would arrive at Hope Bank warm and dry, and it was light enough to stuff into her saddlebag, ready for the return journey, or… she shivered. Should she go to Brewster's farm, or should she wait for a better day? When she had tried to call Tanya last night there had been no answer. What did that mean? Maybe she and her parents were away on one of their many trips. An image of Typhoon's beautiful head slid into her mind. No, she decided, she would go and see him today. The decision left a gurgling flutter lodged beneath her breastbone.

By the time she arrived at Hope Bank, the weather had, if anything, worsened. She parked her bicycle and walked across the yard, head lowered against the rain. The sound of voices just up ahead took her attention and she peered into the misty deluge.

"I'll get him this time," roared Robert Ashton.

He was standing in the corner, wet hair plastered to his head and arms outspread as Bobby's small, shaggy shape charged toward him.

"I'll kill the little monster," he bellowed, right as the bold Shetland barged him easily out of the way.

"That's the third time he's done that," wailed Laura as Cass approached.

"The vet's here to give him his tetanus shot," explained Robert tersely.

"Or not," giggled Laura, watching Bobby disappear around the corner in a series of bucks.

"Maybe we'd better just forget it, Rob?" suggested the vet, Bill Skinner, already packing numerous bottles and boxes into a dark blue hatchback. "I've done all the rest and I'll get him next time I'm here."

He slammed the back door of his car, a broad grin lighting up his plain, pale face. "The little horror is indestructible, anyway."

"Dad's only weak spot," remarked Laura with a smile as the vet clambered in and started the engine.

Bill wound down his window and leaned out, his red hair the only bright color in the misty morning. "See you,"

he called. "Give me a call when you've caught up with him and I'll stop by."

Responding with a half-wave, Robert stalked off, muttering something about paperwork.

Laura grimaced apologetically. "He always goes off to do his paperwork when he's angry," she explained.

Silas, who had been watching the whole proceedings with barely controlled mirth, stepped forward as the vet's car roared off down the lane. "I'll go and get a bucket," he offered, already marching off in the direction of the feed room. "He'll be here like a shot now, you'll see."

Sure enough, with just one good rattle, Bobby appeared around the corner again, trotting happily toward them, ears sharply pricked. "I'm sure he's laughing at us," giggled Laura as he dived his head into the bucket, allowing Silas to slip the head collar over his ears. "Come on, Cass, you can help me muck out the four blocks."

Cass heaved soiled straw into her wheelbarrow, working on auto-pilot as she carefully shook out the clean golden strands and patted them down into a perfect bed while her whole head buzzed with excitement.

"Are you all right?" asked Laura. She pushed her loaded wheelbarrow across the yard toward the muckheap. "You seem a bit... spaced out, I suppose."

Cass grinned. "I was just thinking about Typhoon and the cross-country competition."

Laura rolled her eyes. "Don't even go there," she cried. "I told you that he was total lunatic. That, I think, is an experience best forgotten."

"Yeah, but that's just it," sighed Cass, dropping the handles of her wheelbarrow. "I had a kind of dream, after the... accident. It was so real..."

"Look." Laura gave the younger girl her full attention, a worried frown creasing her forehead. "You had a fall, that's all, and you probably got a concussion. Your mind can do weird things, you know, and any... dream, or whatever it was you had, really is best forgotten."

"I guess you're right," sighed Cass. "So you don't think I should go and try riding him again?"

"Jumping off a cliff would probably be more sensible," advised Laura.

"And a lot less scary," smiled Cass.

Having given Laura the excuse that she had to be home early, Cass pedaled down the road just before lunch and thought about their conversation. She had a lot of respect for Laura, but this time she really couldn't agree with her. Riding Typhoon or jumping off a cliff... where had her sense of adventure gone? Anyway, wasn't she the one who always used to say that there was a way to reach every horse, if you just had the patience to find it?

What was it that Silas always told them? "There are no bad horses, just bad people handling them." Maybe she *owed* it to Ty to try and work out his problem.

Suddenly her mind went into overdrive as she imagined herself bonding with the big black Thoroughbred; for there *was* a way, she was sure of it. All she had to do was find it.

Just up ahead of her now she could see the square white house that overlooked the old-fashioned farmyard at Brewster's and the gray shiny roofs of the low stone buildings surrounding it. Would he be inside, she wondered, or turned out in the paddock? Her heart pounded and she slowed down, breathing deeply. Well, there was only one way to find out.

✸ ✸ ✸ ✸ ✸

Cass saw Typhoon's elegant head as soon as she entered the yard. He was peering over his half door, huge dark eyes shining. Her heart did a long slow flip, and the image of a face flashed immediately into her mind, like a picture from a TV screen. M… Michael Miller, the boy from her dream, how could she have ever believed that she could forget him?

Something trembled deep inside her, something right at her core. But even if it *had* been some kind of sign, what was she supposed to do about it? Typhoon snorted, turning his attention to the young girl who walked slowly toward him. Did he remember too? She held out her hand and he snuffled against it, the bond between them swelling as she breathed in his scent.

"We'll find a way, Ty," she murmured, pressing her face against the silky softness of his nose. "You are the one that counts, not some imaginary person from a stupid dream."

"Who is an imaginary person from a stupid dream?" remarked a high-pitched reedy voice and Cass looked around awkwardly to see a tiny, straight-backed, elderly lady leading two large black, white and tan sheepdogs.

A flood of color rushed from her neck to her hair roots. "Oh… I'm sorry. I just stopped by to see Typhoon. Do you know if Tanya is around?"

The old lady snorted, her dark eyes sparkling angrily. "Tanya is never around," she announced, motioning the dogs to sit. They lowered themselves obediently to the ground and she looked sternly across at Cass. "Now," she insisted. "Tell me about this dream of yours."

"Well…" Cass looked down at her feet. "I rode him, you know, in the cross-country competition…"

"Oh, I know all about that," she cut in. "I'm Tanya's grandmother. Now tell me… about the dream."

"Everyone says it was just a concussion," mumbled Cass, backtracking. "But…"

"Look." The old lady took her arm. "Come into the tack room where it's dry and you can tell me all about it."

CHAPTER 6

Having someone actually take an interest in her story, without immediately discounting it as a weird concussed dream, was, for Cass, like opening a floodgate. She perched on the edge of a paint-splattered wooden chair, fingers tightly clenched and muscles taut as bowstrings. Where to begin?

Mabel Bell smiled encouragingly, and the expression of concentrated interest on her lined face brought such a surge of relief that it flooded through Cass's whole body, triggering a torrent of words with which she relived, yet again, her terrifyingly real experience.

"… So suddenly we were back on the cross-country course and some woman was telling me that I'd fallen," she finally finished, waiting cautiously for the old lady's reaction.

Mabel, sitting just opposite in composed silence with the dogs at her feet, placed her fingers over her lips, looking thoughtful. "I've seen a lot of things in my time," she began, "so I've learned never to discount anything. I can see why they say that you must just have had a concussion and maybe that really is the case, but keep your mind open. If your experience *was* some kind of premonition, then I'm sure that somehow you will get the chance to warn this Michael Miller. Things have a way of working out in life, you'll see. Watch for signs and don't discount anything."

"Mother, what are you doing?" called a loud, impatient male voice, and Cass looked through the open tack room door to see Paul Bell, Tanya's father, approaching from across the yard with the long, purposeful strides she remembered from the day of the cross-country event.

He stepped inside, filling the small room. He was still wearing the expensive dark coat and had an air of authority, she noted, but there was also a softness in his eyes as he looked at his mother. "Come on," he urged, taking her arm as she rose awkwardly to her feet. "You are soaked through. I told you that Tanya would walk the dogs for you later on."

"I've been talking to this young lady," announced Mabel, smiling across at Cass with misty eyes.

"Sorry she bothered you," he apologized, taking the dog leads in one hand while drawing his mother gently off across the yard with the other. "She doesn't see very well, I'm afraid, and she gets a little confused nowadays. Don't take any notice of her."

"She seemed very sensible to me," insisted Cass, feeling a sudden surge of pity for the strange old lady.

"Oh, she has her lucid moments," he explained. "I'll get her inside now. Are you here to see Tanya?"

"If she's around," replied Cass eagerly. Truth was she had been inspired by Mabel Bell's advice. At least *she* had listened, and who knows? Maybe it *was* more than just a dream. Anyway, as the old lady said, if it was meant to be then something would surely happen and she would just have to wait and see.

"She's probably in the house. I'll tell her that you're here," he promised. "And thank you for listening to mother."

It was strange, reflected Cass, slipping into Typhoon's stable to wait for Tanya, how people seemed to behave totally different depending on the situation. On the day of the cross-country event Paul Bell had seemed pompous and overbearing, but today, with his elderly mother, he came across as gracious and kind. Maybe she just brought out the best in him.

Typhoon lowered his head to nuzzle her, showing none of his explosive tendencies now. Maybe he too behaved differently depending on the circumstances, maybe he remembered their experience together and… just maybe… *she* brought out the best in him. Oh, how she hoped so!

Tanya's tall slim figure appeared just five minutes later, walking hurriedly across the yard with short, urgent steps, her hands clenching and unclenching nervously.

"Am I glad to see you," she cried with genuine delight as Cass peered out over Typhoon's half door.

Cass grinned, pleased at her reaction. "I tried to call…" she began awkwardly.

"I felt so bad," went on Tanya. "You know… after… I mean… They said that you had a concussion and couldn't be disturbed."

"Who said?" Suddenly Cass was on her guard. "No one told me that you'd called."

Tanya shrugged. "Oh, I don't know, I called three times and a woman answered. She thanked me for calling, but said that that you weren't up to talking on the phone."

"My grandmother," cried Cass. "She worries, that's all, and she was probably terrified that I was going to try riding Typhoon again."

"And are you?"

Tanya's eyes looked huge in her pale, gaunt face as she waited for the other girl's reply. It came automatically. "Of course I am."

"Today?"

Cass ran her hand down the big black horse's silky neck, and suddenly decided. "Yes, why not?"

"He hasn't been ridden since… since the cross-country incident," admitted Tanya. "My grandmother said that I should just get on with it but I was too scared. It's all right for her, she used to be a brilliant rider before…"

"I met your grandmother," cut in Cass. "She listened to me."

Tanya smiled. "She does sometimes, and today she must have felt really good because she walked the dogs for the first time in weeks. She lives in the small stone cottage just down the road, next door to Dad and me."

"Oh," remarked Cass. "I just kind of assumed that she lived in the white house over there.

Tanya shook her head. "She used to, but she sold the place and moved into the cottage when my grandfather died. Tom Bradley farms here now. He helps me to look after Ty, or rather…" A dull flush colored her pale cheeks. "I suppose you could say that it's me who helps him. To be totally honest, I've hardly been to the yard since the cross-country."

"And your mother?" Suddenly Cass felt that she needed to find out as much as she could about Tanya, as if knowing her better would make it easier to understand her horse.

"She lives in Hastings," she replied, in a flat, disinterested tone. "Gran is the one who always looked after me, until…"

A heavy silence slid between the two girls for a moment and then Tanya let out a sigh. "She had a stroke," she went on sadly, looking down at her long, slim fingers. "And she hasn't been the same since. Some days she's just like her old self and then she just kind of drifts away."

"Well, I thought she was great," cried Cass. "She made a lot of sense."

"She scolds about Ty sometimes," admitted Tanya. "You know, for not coming to see him. I know it's no excuse, but I'm just so scared, and the stupid thing is that I really do love the crazy horse."

74

"That's okay." Suddenly Cass wanted so much to help the tall, fragile girl who appeared to have everything and yet was too afraid to make the most of her opportunities. Maybe it wasn't all about money after all. "I'm here to help you with him now, aren't I? I'm sure that together we can work something out."

Tanya's expression said it all.

It felt strange to be putting her foot into Typhoon's stirrup again, Cass noted while mounting the excitable Thoroughbred half an hour later.

"Maybe we should have lunged him first," remarked Tanya, desperately chewing her bottom lip.

"Well, you said that he'd been turned in the field everyday, so he should be okay," insisted Cass with a show of confidence that she was far from feeling. Typhoon sidled beneath her as she sank into the saddle, and she reached down to pat his neck. "It's okay, boy. Remember me?" she murmured, taking up the reins.

Ahead of her his two black ears were sharply pointed forward, his mane rippling down his neck as she asked him to walk on. He responded immediately, lowering his head to mouth on the bit, and suddenly her confidence soared. "Can I take him in the field over there?" she cried.

"Take him anywhere you like," replied Tanya with a broad grin.

This was different from before; Cass could feel it at once. The big black horse was calmer and more self-assured, and he responded to her every touch instinctively. "It's like riding on air," she cried as he cantered around in effortless circles.

"He's never like that with me," groaned Tanya. "I think he knows I'm nervous."

Cass reined in, allowing Typhoon to walk back to the gate on a loose rein. "That's just it," she said, pulling up next to where Tanya was perched on the fence. "He's nervous too; he was terrified at the cross-country event. I can see that now, and my nerves were all over the place too. The more confident I feel the easier he is to ride; he relaxes when he knows he has someone in charge."

"Well, I'm out, then," sighed Tanya. "Even at the best of times I'm not a confident rider."

"Well, I'd hate for you to sell him," admitted Cass, "but have you ever thought about getting something quieter, a horse you can really enjoy?"

Tanya grinned, her drawn face suddenly brightening. "You know, you might just have given me a really good idea."

Cass was intrigued. "What idea?"

"Come back tomorrow and I'll tell you," promised Tanya. "I'll have to run it by my dad first."

All the way home Cass's mind was whirling. What was Tanya's 'good idea'? Was she going to put Ty on the market and get a new horse, as Cass had suggested? Her heart fell, descending with a thump to the very bottom of her boots. Today she had suddenly realized just how attached to the high-strung Thoroughbred she was, and it went far deeper than just his looks and awesome talent. It was the whole challenge of him, his sensitivity and desperate need of support, the way he responded when he finally gave her his trust. A sob welled up in her throat and she increased her speed, as if the physical pain of effort would fend off the misery that overpowered her. She couldn't let Tanya sell Typhoon, but how could she stop her? It had been her own stupid suggestion in the first place.

❀ ❀ ❀ ❀ ❀

As Sarah Truman watched her granddaughter approach along the road she could see immediately, by the droop of her shoulders, that something was wrong. Her heart fell. Cass was only just recovering from her fall and she still had the headaches following her concussion. The last thing she needed right now was yet another setback.

She hurried over to meet her, noting the red blotches on her tanned face as soon as she burst in through the kitchen door. "Okay, love, tell me what's happened; is it your headache again?"

"No," Cass turned away, heading for the stairs. "It's nothing."

"Cassandra!" Her grandmother was not taking "nothing" for an answer and reluctantly Cass turned back.

"It's nothing, honestly," she insisted, looking down at the floor.

"You've been riding that crazy horse, haven't you?"

Suddenly the floodgates burst open and for the second time that day Cass found herself pouring out her heart. This time, however, it had nothing to do with her weird experience; that was way in the back of her mind.

"Oh Gran, he was so amazing," she cried. "You should have seen him. And he's not bad, he's just nervous and high-strung. We'd have such trust. I know we would do well together, if we only had the time."

Sarah Truman smiled knowingly, putting her concerned comments on hold; her granddaughter's happiness was far more important than her own fears. "And you think that Granddad Bill and I are such old fools now that we can't remember how it was to hope and dream? Look, love, we may worry about you but we would never hold you back from doing something you really want to do. Be careful, that is all we ask."

Cass flushed. "No, of course I know that… and I don't blame you for worrying, it's just… Tanya is going to sell him and I'll never be able to ride him again."

When tears began to slip from beneath Cass's burning eyelids, running down her cheeks in tiny rivers, Sarah stepped forward to give her a quick hug and suddenly realized with a slight sense of shock that her teenage granddaughter was actually taller than she was.

"You are growing up, love," she sighed, realizing that she couldn't protect her forever. "Bad things happen to all of us sometimes, and there are always disappointments in life, no matter who you are, but there are ways to get through them too, if you don't give up. You just have to think positively. Things often have a way of sorting themselves out, you'll see."

Cass gave a watery grin, realizing that Gran was the second old lady to give her that particular piece of advice today. "Thanks, Gran," she murmured. "You're right, and I don't even know for sure that he is for sale yet anyway."

"Well, there you are," responded Sarah. "So worry about it when it happens. Now run along and get changed. Your granddad will be in shortly and you can tell him all about it."

To Cass's delight the sun chose to shine the following morning, putting a whole new face on the day and lightening her mood. She set off early, determined to go and spend some more time with Typhoon that afternoon – after she had finished helping out at the stables, of course. To skip out on her Hope Bank duties without a very good reason was out of the question. Robert and Mollie Ashton, Laura, Jack, old Silas and all the horses tugged at her heartstrings, comfortable and familiar, like a second home and family. She even harbored hopes of working there full time one day, after she finished school, of course, to follow her dream of competing against the best.

Enjoying the feel of the crisp early morning air against her skin, she let her mind wander; she and Typhoon, galloping to success – a dream that she knew full well could never materialize. But what if he was already advertised for sale…? What if… what if… what if? Life was full of what ifs. What if her dream was true? What if she really *was* supposed to warn M… and what if…?

Pushing the negative thoughts from her mind, she focused on the road ahead, breathing in the soft, sweet scents of summer. Overhead the sky was as blue as it could get with just a few cotton candy-type clouds drifting lazily in the gentle breeze. Surely nothing bad could happen on such a glorious day, could it? Anyway, at least she would be able to ride Ty again before he went – obviously such a difficult horse wasn't going to be easy to sell. For now she would just make the most of her opportunity.

Mollie Ashton was the first person Cass saw when she arrived at Hope Bank with her head in the clouds. She was crossing the yard, limping slightly, bright orange tee shirt clashing garishly with her cloud of chestnut curls. When she saw Cass she stopped, throwing back her shoulders and cupping her broad hips firmly with both hands. "Am I glad to see you!"

Unused to quite such an enthusiastic welcome, Cass leaned her bike against the wall and hurried toward her.

"That Jack Donelly has let us down again, I'm afraid," announced Mollie, shaking her head in exasperation. "Only this time it seems that he's not coming back."

"What?"

Cass remembered their last conversation, when Jack told her that he wasn't staying around much longer. She hadn't realized that his departure was to be as sudden as this, however. Unreliable he may be, but he was also charming and good-looking and a very talented rider, and she couldn't imagine Hope Bank without him.

"I can't believe that he has actually left... for good... just like that," she cried.

"*Just* like that," echoed Mollie. "Seemingly, and to be fair he did sound sorry, but he appears to have gotten a better offer that he just can't refuse."

"Billy Bowen was always after him," reflected Cass.

"Well, whatever," went on Mollie. "But maybe it will all turn out for the best, anyway, as he *was* always letting us down. Fortunately, Robert has already found a replacement, or at least I hope he has."

Cass nodded, frowning. "When you think about it, I suppose Jack was always calling with some excuse. So, who is this new guy, and when does he start?"

Mollie shrugged. "Rob met him at a show the other day. He might be totally hopeless, of course, but he's supposed to be a good rider, and he's looking for work in a competition yard. We're hoping that he can start as soon as possible."

Cass felt a sudden wave of disappointment at the thought of never seeing Jack's handsome face again, or being at the mercy of his constant jokes. Truth be known, both she and Laura were half in love with his roguish charm.

"We'll miss Jack, though," she sighed.

Mollie's hazel eyes twinkled. "Oh, I think that we all know how you and Laura felt about him," she laughed, "but this new boy is younger, closer to your own age."

Cass brightened. "Where *is* Laura?" she asked eagerly.

"Mucking out the three block," responded Mollie. "And don't you two spend all morning gossiping."

"We won't," promised Cass, already heading off across the yard.

By the time Mollie called them all in for lunch Silas and the two girls had finished all the main yard work while Robert Ashton rode the horses he had in for schooling. "Why don't you go out for a trail ride with Laura this afternoon?" he suggested to Cass as they all walked across the yard together toward the house. "That new bay needs some exercise, and Laura hasn't worked Steel yet."

"Oh yes," cried Laura eagerly. "You'll love Sunny. I rode him yesterday; he's a real character."

Images of Typhoon's lovely face flashed into Cass's mind. For the first time ever, she did not eagerly grab the opportunity to ride a new horse. "Thanks, that would be great, but I have to go early today."

"Well, we'll hurry lunch and get straight out, then," exclaimed Laura. "We could go up the bridle path and gallop across the pasture. We can be back by two."

Delighted at the opportunity to have what appeared to be the best of both worlds, Cass grinned, nodding eagerly. "Come on then," she cried. "Let's hurry."

The chunky bay gelding, Sunny, proved to be a fun ride, fun enough to even take Cass's mind off both her ever-present ominous dream *and* the spirited black gelding that had stolen her heart. It wasn't until she and Laura were heading homeward again in companionable silence that her worries came filtering back.

The soothing clop of hooves filled her ears, a gentle

breeze caressed her face and the horrors of the cross-country day seemed to belong to another life, lived by someone else. Somehow, on this very ordinary, happy day, it seemed safe to talk about her fears.

"Do you remember the story I told you about Typhoon bolting with me and what happened after?" she tentatively began.

Laura stopped humming and looked across at Cass curiously. "You mean your concussion and that crazy dream?"

"Do you really think that it was a dream, though? What if it was real?"

Laura laughed out loud, urging Steel into a trot. "Of course it was a dream," she chortled. "Honestly, Cass, sometimes I think that you live in Cloud-cuckoo-land."

"I've been back to ride him, you know," blurted out Cass. "Typhoon, I mean."

"Now I know that you're in Cloud-cuckoo-land," cried Laura, reining in again. "He didn't finish you off on the cross-country, so you decided to let him have another try, is that it?"

"No," Cass flew to Typhoon's defense at once. "He's just nervous, that's all."

"And crazy," grinned Laura.

"Sensitive," declared Cass, smiling back.

"The trouble with you," grumbled Laura, "is that you can't resist a challenge. I suppose that's where you are hurrying off to this afternoon, right? Going to ride him again?"

"If he hasn't been sold already," sighed Cass.

Laura just shook her head hopelessly. "Well, let's just hope he has."

Tanya was already waiting impatiently when Cass eventually

arrived at Brewster's farm; her pale face was bright with excitement and she jumped eagerly from foot to foot.

"What's going on?" asked Cass. What happened?"

Tanya squirmed, clasping her hands tightly together. "You know what I said yesterday, about my idea?"

Cass froze. "To sell Typhoon, you mean," she cried, her heart sinking.

Tanya frowned. "Sell him… what? No, of course not."

A prickle of excitement bubbled up Cass's throat. "Well, what was your idea, then?"

Tanya smiled triumphantly, holding the moment. "I'm going to move him to the boarding stable at Hope Bank," she announced, "and then you can help me with him. Actually, my dad says that I may even be able to get another quieter horse, too, and maybe you could take over Typhoon's schooling. If you want to, that is."

"If I want to!?" Hope soared like a caged bird set free. "And you're definitely not selling him?"

Tanya shook her head, smiling happily. "No, of course not. Not if you'll help me!"

"As if you need to ask that," grinned Cass, grabbing Tanya by both hands. "I'll do all the work, I promise, and I'll help you with your new horse if you get one! But will your dad *really* do that? Let you have two horses at the stable, I mean?"

Tanya shrugged. "My dad is so busy working that he'll do anything just to keep me busy and out of trouble. And I have to look after Gran, of course, because he never has the time."

"I'll help with your grandmother, too," offered Cass. "You know, walking the dogs, and stuff like that. I think she's great."

"She is great," agreed Tanya, her eyes softening. "And

what Dad doesn't realize is that I'll always look after her, no matter what. Anyway, come on, he's already called Hope Bank and Robert Ashton said that we can take Ty over there this afternoon. Dad says he'll deliver him as soon as he gets home from work, if we have everything ready, of course."

While Tanya hurried away to get all the tack, leaving her to sort out feed buckets and rugs, Cass headed off at once to where Typhoon was staring out over his half door. She felt as if she was in a dream; an impossible, unbelievable dream. At last she had the chance she had been waiting for, and she was determined to make the most of it.

"You and me, Ty," she whispered, pressing her cheek against the velvety softness of his nose, not noticing the strange distant expression in his huge, dark eyes as he stared toward the horizon.

CHAPTER 7

As the Bell's huge silver four-wheel drive and matching trailer swung into the yard at Hope Bank a shiver of excitement rippled up Cass's spine. She felt as if this was the start of a whole new phase to her life, a real opportunity at last.

She scrambled eagerly out the back door to be met by Laura, who stared at her in amazement. "Don't tell me that Typhoon is the new horse I'm supposed to meet," she gasped, her forehead puckering into a concerned frown. "And I suppose you're going to ride him? Are you sure about this, Cass?"

Cass grinned, throwing back her shoulders. "I have never been surer of anything in my whole life," she announced, reaching up to open the catches that secured the trailer ramp.

Laura placed a hand on her arm, getting her attention. "Well, be careful, at least. You know what he's capable of."

For a fleeting moment Cass held her gaze. "Don't worry," she smiled. "I've learned my lesson and I promise not to take any chances."

"When *don't* you take chances, Cass Truman?" giggled Laura as the side ramp came down with gentle thud. "Anyway, don't say that I didn't warn you… and if you ever do get him trained then you're welcome to come to some shows with me."

Cass ran up the ramp to where Typhoon waited impatiently. "Thanks," she responded, smiling so broadly that it felt as if her face might crack, and in that moment, she felt as if life could not get any better. Just a short time later, however she was not quite so sure.

❀ ❀ ❀ ❀ ❀

Typhoon had been allotted a box at the very end of the row in front of the barn. He stepped nervously inside with one forefoot, snorting loudly, while Cass hung determinedly onto the lead rope.

"He's always like this in a strange place," remarked Tanya, stepping back out of harm's way as the big black horse pulled backwards, almost jamming Cass in the doorway.

"And how long does he usually take to settle down?" Cass asked cautiously, turning him around to face the narrow entrance again. He shied violently, pulling back, and a quiver of concern turned her mouth dry.

"Oh," Tanya shrugged, happy just to observe. "A few days, I guess."

"Come on, boy," begged Cass, but the nervous gelding wasn't cooperating, and spun around again just as Robert Ashton appeared from the direction of the house. Cass's heart fell. What if he told Tanya's dad that Typhoon was too much for her, and he decided to sell him after all?

To her relief, though, he just smiled encouragingly. "You've got yourself a challenge there," he remarked, reaching for the lead rope. "Here, let me help."

Cass gave up reluctantly, watching in awe as the tall, white-haired man ran his hand down Typhoon's face, murmuring reassuringly under his breath until eventually the black gelding lowered his head, blowing softly through his nostrils.

"You see," he told her, handing the lead rope back. "Just take your time and stay calm, give him a bit of confidence. He's a lovely horse, worth spending time on. Patience, that's the key."

Cass caught Tanya's eye, a surge of pride turning her cheeks pink. "He has a great jump, too," she told him, excitement bubbling inside her.

"Well, get the flat work right first, and then we'll see what he can do," he promised. "Oh, and by the way, did you enjoy riding Sunny this afternoon?"

"He was great," nodded Cass, a pinprick of melancholy penetrating her euphoria as she remembered that the generous little bay horse's days at Hope Bank were numbered. "Do you have a buyer for him yet?"

"No," He reached out to run his hand down Typhoon's quivering quarters. "But he'll be easy to sell. He's anyone's ride, unlike this guy here. I'm definitely glad that *he's* not here for me to try and sell. Anyway, I'd better get going. I'll see you two young ladies later. And for heaven's sakes, be careful."

As he turned to walk off across the yard Cass thought how aptly named the sweet bay gelding was. Sunny by name and Sunny by nature, she mused... Of course, that was it!

"You should buy him, Tanya," she cried, her tone high-pitched with excitement. "Sunny, I mean. It's the perfect solution. He is a total darling, and he's right here under your very nose – if you're serious about buying another horse, that is."

Tanya nodded eagerly. "Of course I'm serious! Just tell me when I can see him."

Overhearing the conversation, Robert Ashton stopped and looked back, his dark eyes glinting at the chance of a possible deal. "You can see him right now if you like, or at least just as soon as Cass here gets this black monster into his box."

As if on cue, at that exact moment, Typhoon lowered his head and rushed in through the door, almost knocking her down in his haste. She shut it firmly behind him, sliding the bolt with a sigh of relief. "Why don't you two go now," she suggested. "And I'll join you in a minute, once I've settled him in."

To Cass's relief that didn't prove to be quite as arduous a task as she had anticipated; as Robert strode off across the yard, followed eagerly by Tanya, Typhoon was already munching on his hay net, happy now that he was through the offending door. Cass patted his neck and adjusted his rug. "Well, boy," she murmured. "We've got our chance now, so let's not blow it this time."

For a moment, the big black horse looked right at her with a strange, distant expression that gave her goose bumps – as if he had his own private agenda. She closed her eyes, fighting off the terrifying memories of the cross-country troubles. That was all behind her now – despite the nightmares that still haunted her sleep and the fears that woke her at the dead of night. The past was gone, and she had to focus on what really mattered, the glorious future that stretched out before them, she and Typhoon. Or at least that was what she had to try and convince herself of.

By the time Cass eventually joined Tanya at Sunny's stable, Robert Ashton already had him out on the yard. His curly tipped ears were pricked appealingly and he nuzzled Tanya gently, almost as if begging her to buy him.

"You see," remarked Robert, his white head bobbing earnestly as he went into full sales mode. "He has a lovely nature, and of course he's only six years old so he has his whole future ahead of him. Do you want me to trot him for you?"

Tanya nodded eagerly, flashing Cass an excited smile. "He is so gorgeous," she sighed as the chunky bay gelding trotted nimbly across the yard.

"He almost looks as if he has a smile on his face," agreed Cass.

"That's what I love most about him," agreed Tanya. "His cute face with that lovely white snip right between his nostrils and the tiny white star."

"Well, you'd better have a ride on him, then," suggested Cass. "And have you even asked how much he is?"

"I'll get Dad to speak to Mr. Ashton about that," declared Tanya. "But I would love to try him, if that's all right, and guess what?"

"What?" smiled Cass.

"I don't even feel at all nervous about it!"

Robert was handing her the lead rope and heading off to get Sunny's tack before she had even finished speaking.

"And I'll tell you one thing for sure," Cass told her. "You won't be disappointed. He's like riding on a great comfy, bouncy cushion."

Cass walked slowly homeward later that evening, her mind reeling. *Were* the events of the day real, or could they have all been just a crazy dream from which she would awaken at any moment, like the cross-country event reversed?

Tanya and Sunny had clicked just as soon as Tanya sat in the saddle; you could see the bond between them forming with every stride he took. It seemed impossible to believe, though, that she could have found a new horse already and that Typhoon was actually here, at Hope Bank. And what if Paul Bell insisted that his daughter should sell Ty now after all? Words were just words, and the promise had only been made to get her to help Tanya. If Tanya bought Sunny, then she wasn't going to need Cass's help anymore. She also wasn't going to need Typhoon any more, and to be fair, why should they keep a horse just for

91

her? He had settled down so well at his new stable that she didn't think she could bear it if everything fell through. She took a breath, increasing her pace, suddenly needing the comfortable stability of her grandmother's understanding smile. Surely all her dreams couldn't come crashing down now, could they?

Despite her initial fears, it seemed that for Cass, over the next week or so, life could not get any better. Typhoon was still far from easy, of course, and the trips through his dreaded doorway didn't improve much, but she felt that the bond between them was growing daily. She took no chances, remembering the horror when he bolted with her, but the Typhoon that ran off into the woods seemed a million miles away.

Tanya was so busy now with Sunny that she gave Cass free rein and, to her relief, nothing was mentioned again about him having to be sold. She rode him for hours, often all the way to Tall Trees to help Anna, whose confidence with Duke was improving all the time. Sometimes she even dared to venture right up the pasture; in fact, it began to feel as if Ty really was her very own horse. In the back of her mind though, darkening her dreams, lurked the awareness that he could be taken from her at any moment.

Determinedly she tried to ignore her fears and live for the moment – after all, it was probably the nearest she was ever going to get to owning her own horse, so she may as well make the most of it, and Paul Bell *had* promised to keep him for a little while longer if she helped Tanya with Sunny. To Cass, that was a small price for having the opportunity to train the most talented horse she had ever ridden. Actually, he was the only horse she had ever had the opportunity to be totally in charge of. Tomorrow's tears would come soon enough, she decided, and she would just live for today.

It was a bright, early morning in midsummer and Cass had just started mucking out Sunny's stable when Tanya burst in through the doorway with the news that was to change her whole life. Cass looked up at her friend cautiously; it was difficult now to associate the suntanned, bright-eyed girl who was smiling at her so eagerly with the pale, willowy, nervous youngster that she had first seen on the day she took Duke to the show.

"My dad had a thought," announced Tanya, her voice high pitched with excitement.

Cass's heart did a long, slow flip and she carefully patted down the last unruly piece of straw before responding. She had come to realize that both Tanya and her father liked to act spontaneously, and who knew what they might have dreamed up this time.

"What kind of a thought?" she asked cautiously, placing her fork against the wall.

For just a moment Tanya hesitated, holding onto the moment. "He wants *you* to buy Typhoon," she announced.

A cold trickle of fear made Cass's heart beat overtime; suddenly her dream was evaporating before her very eyes. "But I can't afford him…"

Tanya smiled, waving both hands. "No, don't worry. He doesn't actually want any money! The thing is, I can't always come to see to Sunny – oh, it's okay now during the vacation, but once I'm back at school I'll have to look after Gran, and my school is miles away, so we thought that maybe you could buy Ty, but pay for him by helping with Sunny. What do you think? We can work out a real price and everything."

"What do I think?"

A ripple of tears streamed down Cass's cheeks and choked-up throat.

"I think that you must be my fairy godmother."

It wasn't until much later that reality hit her. "I don't want to look a gift horse in the mouth, so to speak," she admitted to Laura. "But even if it does work out, how am I going to pay for Ty's keep?"

Ever practical, Laura pursed her lips. "Well, first you need to go home and tell your grandparents, I'm sure they'll help you out a little. And I have another idea, but I'll have to speak to Dad first."

Cass was on tenterhooks all day, unable to concentrate, even when riding Typhoon who, to her dismay, reverted to form by bolting with her along the road. She eventually pulled him up outside the gates to Hope Bank, her face bright pink with exertion and her heart racing.

"Lost a bit of concentration, huh?" called Robert Ashton, from across the yard.

"Yes, but it was my fault," insisted Cass.

"You're right it was your fault," he agreed. "You can't be caught half asleep on a horse like that. Anyway, come to my office when you've put him away. I have a proposition for you."

Cass's fingers fumbled with the leather buckles as she un-tacked Typhoon. What did Robert Ashton mean, "a proposition"? Her whole life seemed to be going so crazy at the moment that she had even managed to push the cross-country day horrors to the back of her mind.

Twenty minutes later she burst into the small wooden shed that served as an office and stopped dead inside the doorway, her heart firmly trapped in her mouth. "You wanted to see me?"

Robert looked around, putting down his pen and pushing a pile of horse magazines onto the floor before motioning her to sit down on the chair he had cleared.

"Right," he announced, sitting back with his hands behind his head. "How would you feel about working here properly, for Typhoon's stabling?"

"How do I feel?" blurted out Cass.

"Yes, that *was* the question," he responded. "You would have to work hard and put in real hours. None of this coming and going whenever you please."

"So you would keep him here for nothing?" she gasped.

"No." He frowned, glancing down at the sheet of paper in front of him. "Here, I've written it all down for you. "If you come every weekend, first thing, then you'll earn enough to pay for his actual board – that's his stable and turnout, one bale of shavings a week and unrestricted haylage. All you would have to pay for is his hard feed and shoeing and worming, and the vet, of course."

"And you would really do that for me?"

Robert looked into Cass's ecstatic face in exasperation. "I don't just hand out favors, you know," he assured her. "I can't afford to. You would be helping *me* out. Heaven knows we're short staffed already. Anyway!" He looked at her brightly. "The new groom starts next week and that should make things easier. So, what do you think?"

"What do I think?"

"That *was* the question…"

"I think yes please, yes please, yes please!"

Reaching out, Robert took her hand, shaking it firmly. "Okay, it's a deal, then."

"A deal," echoed Cass.

❁ ❁ ❁ ❁ ❁

As she rode toward Tall Trees later that afternoon, her head firmly fixed in the clouds, a tiny niggle of worry began to worm its way like a canker into her happiness, for it had always seemed to her in the past that it was just when everything seemed to be going right that something always went wrong.

She shook off the feeling impatiently. After all, what could go wrong? Typhoon was improving every day – Laura had even promised to let her take him to the next novice show they did, and now, unbelievably, it seemed that she was actually going to own him, so no one could take him away from her, ever. In fact things really were turning out perfectly, weren't they?

Out of the blue a shadowy scene flashed into her mind. The horror on the young man's face as his lovely gray horse careered down the steep incline and the tombstone loomed out at her, blocking her way.

Concentrating on the road ahead she tried to blank out the unwanted memories, ignoring the heavy thud of her heart. It had all just been a stupid dream, she was sure of it now, a dream that belonged in the past. The future was all that really mattered, hers and Typhoon's.

CHAPTER 8

Typhoon's ears were pricked before her, so high that she could barely see over them. "Put your leg on," yelled Robert Ashton, "and get him a bit more around."

Cass did as she was told, and as the big black horse lowered his head she felt a surge of power beneath her. "That's the sort of canter you need," cried Robert. "Now take him to the parallel and don't lose your rhythm."

Cass turned the corner, keeping her inside leg on.

"Keep your eye on the fence."

The red and white parallel loomed before her, nerves fluttered on tiny wings and she took a breath, channeling them into determination. Euphoria rose like a tide as Typhoon left the ground with an awesome surge of power, landing effortlessly, as if on cotton candy, and cantered forwards, his head between his knees. Cass stood up in the stirrups, punching the air, unable to contain whoops of joy.

"That will do for now," grinned Robert. "He has some potential, I'll grant you that. A good horse should leave the ground with a thud and land in silence, my dad always used to say, and he certainly does that."

"He's just amazing," cried Cass, collapsing onto his neck.

"Well, don't get too confident," advised Robert. "You haven't taken him anywhere yet, and look what happened last time. But I'll tell you what."

He stopped in his tracks, shielding his eyes from the sun as he looked up at the slightly built girl whose brown eyes gleamed as brightly as her chestnut curls. "You can take him in the trailer when we do the novice show in Ripton, if you like. It's a couple of weeks away still, so you'll have plenty more time to practice."

The expression on Cass's face required no answer.

"I'll take that as a yes," laughed Robert, walking away. "Oh, and by the way, Jack's replacement starts tomorrow, so hopefully you and Laura should have a bit less to do."

As Cass dismounted from Typhoon and ran up his stirrups she realized just how appealing that idea was. Never one to be scared of hard work, she had to admit that the last couple of weeks had been just a bit too much – on some days there had hardly even been enough time to ride. She wondered what the new boy would be like while taking Ty's reins over his head to lead him back to his stable. Would he be going with them to the Ripton show? Her stomach gurgled. "We're going to a show, boy," she announced. "And you're going in the novice jumping class."

Typhoon blew through his nostrils, lunging for his hay net as Cass went to undo his girth, and she took hold of his reins, drawing him around to face her. "You won't let me down this time, though, will you?"

The big black gelding shook his head, stamping his foot at an annoying fly, and she ran her hand down his damp neck. "Is that a promise?"

"He can't speak, you know," giggled Laura from over the half door. "Here, pass me your tack and I'll put it away for you. By the way, I heard that Dad offered to take you to Ripton with us. Are you sure you're ready for that?"

"Only one way to find out," smiled Cass. "But you should have seen him jump this afternoon."

Laura grinned. "I heard, and to be honest, I have to admit that even Dad seemed impressed for once; the only problem is that you *do* have to get around the whole course without him bolting off, you know."

Cass's initial frown turned into a giggle as she saw

the humor in her friend's eyes. "Well, we have to start somewhere, don't we? And at least this time you'll be there to pick up the pieces."

Laura heaved the saddle onto her hip. "Oh, and by the way, speaking of difficult horses, how are you progressing with the mighty Duke?"

"He's doing great," responded Cass with a broad grin. "Anna seems to have gotten some confidence at last, so I think she'll definitely be keeping him."

"And Tanya has totally bonded with Sunny," Laura reminded her. "So it seems that *you* are quite the little matchmaker."

Cass shrugged. "Not really. I was just in the right place at the right time, I suppose."

Laura hesitated, glancing away and then back again, as if undecided about whether or not to go on. When she did speak her voice was hurried and a dark flush flooded her cheeks, "And have you got over all that other stuff now, you know, those crazy stories you used to tell me about your... premonition?"

Cass squared her shoulders, smiling determinedly. "If you mean my concussion, then yes... I really think that I have."

"We were all worried about you, you know," remarked Laura, meeting her gaze squarely.

"Well, you don't need to worry anymore," reassured Cass. "I hit my head and had some crazy ideas, and now all I want to think about is the future."

"And the Ripton show," finished Laura with a broad grin.

"*Mainly* the Ripton show," agreed Cass.

The first thing Cass saw of Hope Bank's newest staff member the next morning was the back of his head over the horsebox partition. He had been due to arrive at ten, but when an elderly green and gold truck rolled into the yard just before half past nine, she and Laura, who were still finishing mucking out, both put down their tools and hurried eagerly outside, feigning disinterest but with curiosity in their eyes.

Robert Ashton lowered the ramp and a cloud of steam temporarily camouflaged the occupants. "He always travels badly," explained a muffled voice from beyond the impatient thudding of hooves.

Cass peered up the ramp to see a tall, dark haired figure untying the lead rope of a large gray horse. It nickered loudly, tossing its head, and a prickle of discomfort brought a shiver to her limbs as he turned to lead it down the ramp. Her heart thudded beneath her ribcage as she tried to get a glimpse of his face, but just as he appeared on the ramp Robert Ashton stepped forward, blocking her view. The dull thud of hooves penetrated her confusion, followed by a sharp clip-clopping sound as metal met concrete.

"Well, girls," announced Robert, stepping back. "Meet…"

The new hire stepped forward, towering over her, dark sparkling eyes, suntanned skin and a smile that reached into her very core.

"Michael Miller," he said, his voice deep and vibrant. "At your service."

For Cass it felt as if the whole world was closing in on her, taking her breath and rendering all her senses useless. Her legs turned to jelly, her heart pounded in her ears and suddenly the ground was rising up to meet her.

It was Robert Ashton who jumped forward to break her fall, grabbing her shoulders and hauling her back onto her feet. "Get your mother," he told Laura, who rushed off immediately to do as she was told.

"You're okay," Robert reassured her, and Cass managed a weak, shaky smile. "Sorry, it's just –"

"I'm not that scary, am I?" smiled Michael.

She ran his name around inside her head, Michael, Michael Miller; the name that had been burned into her every waking thought for weeks, the name that had haunted her dreams and turned them into nightmares.

"Do you think that I should call the doctor?" asked Robert urgently as his wife hurried toward them, her limp more pronounced than usual and her cheeks still pink from the stove. Laura followed closely, her face starkly pale in contrast.

"I'm fine now, honestly," reassured Cass.

"Well, you don't look alright," declared Mollie Ashton, placing a comforting arm around her shoulders, and for just a moment Cass leaned against the warm softness of her ample figure, trying to steady her breathing.

"I'll call her grandparents," offered Laura.

"No! Honestly," Cass pulled herself up straight, trying to control the shivering in her limbs. "I really am fine now, please don't worry."

"Well, I think that you should go home, at least," insisted Robert. "You look like death."

Death! Cass's heart began racing again as the word loomed out at her. The Michael Miller of her dream was real. He was here, in the flesh, looking down at her with burning dark eyes and beside him…

Another image flashed into her mind, a gray horse standing three legged, its once proud head on its knees and beside it, awkwardly slumped in an impossible position…

"Maybe I will go home," she agreed, suddenly unable to cope with the proximity of the young man from her nightmares, the living proof that her gut instincts had been right all along, and that her dream really wasn't a dream at all. So was that the truth? Had her terrifying experience been a premonition of events to come… the premonition of…? She closed her eyes, unable to look at the handsome young man who stared at her with such concern. She had to warn him! But how?

"I'll drive her over," offered Mollie, and Cass shot her a grateful smile, desperately needing time alone with her thoughts, time to try and straighten everything out in her head. If anything could ever be straight again. And what was she going to tell her grandparents?

In the end she decided on the truth, guiltily watching the confused expressions on their loving wrinkled faces as they exchanged a worried glance before ushering her off to bed like a nine-year-old. Unbelievably, she slept.

Sarah Truman placed a gentle hand on her granddaughter's forehead, a shadow dulling the usual brightness of her face.

"Maybe we had better take her to see the doctor?" suggested her husband. "I thought all that wild ranting after the concussion was behind us, but this is crazy."

From behind a comforting veil of sleep, Cass's mind was being haunted by whirling, vague nightmares. The touch of her grandmother's hand brought reality back with a lurch, but she kept her eyes closed, listening to the thoughts of these two sweet people who had nothing but her best interests at heart. If *they* thought that she was crazy, then who could she turn to?

"She seems to think that the new young man at Hope Bank is the same one that haunted her nightmares," sighed Sarah. "That she needs to warn him about something."

"Maybe it's the concussion again and she just needs a sedative to calm her nerves," suggested her husband, shaking his white head in despair. "I'll call for an appointment with Dr. Smith first thing in the morning."

Suddenly, through the cloudy release of slumber, Cass

realized that to burden the old couple with her fears was not only a hopeless waste of time, but also selfish and cruel. Somehow she had to find a way through this on her own since no one was ever going to believe her story.

She opened her eyes, forcing a smile onto her face. "I'm sorry," she groaned, sitting up on the side of the bed. "I think I must just have had a relapse. I'm fine now, honestly."

"And you don't think that this Michael Miller is in danger?" frowned her grandfather.

"No!"

Cass stood up, unable to bear the feelings that were crowding her head. "I think that he must just have looked like the boy from my dream and it gave me a shock, that's all."

Her grandmother was not so easily convinced. "And you are sure about this?"

Cass nodded. "Oh yes. I'll stay here today though, if you think that it's best."

"Well, that just may be a good idea. It's almost midnight," agreed her grandfather.

"And I'll make you hot chocolate to help you get back to sleep again," suggested Sarah Truman with a worried glance at her granddaughter's pale face.

Much to her grandparent's disapproval, Cass set off on her bicycle the next morning, her head still spinning. She had managed to feign normality throughout breakfast, forcing down a piece of toast and smiling with tight, hard lips.

Granddad Bill had put his foot down at first, insisting that she stay at home, but Cass had managed, as usual, to bring them around to her way of thinking. "I really am fine now," she had insisted. "Honestly. And I have Ty to take care of now, not to mention all the other work at Hope Bank."

"Mollie Ashton has already called to say that they

can manage without you if you're still not feeling well," grumbled Sarah, but Cass wouldn't dream of it.

She sat back down at the kitchen table for a moment, trying to put their fears to rest. "Look," she began. "I had that concussion after my fall, and those awful nightmares, you know about that. Then when I saw Michael Miller it shocked me, that's all. He had the same name as the boy in my dream, you see, but of course I realize now that it was just a weird coincidence. Why, when I actually stop and think about it, I can see that he doesn't even look the same."

"But are you are sure?" her grandparents had asked, unconvinced.

"I am *totally* sure," she had declared with a forced grin. "So stop worrying."

Her legs slowed as she approached Hope Bank; suddenly the thought of seeing Michael Miller was just too much to cope with. She had never felt so alone and afraid in her whole life, not to mention desperately worried about M's fate. There, she had thought of him as M again, it made things seem easier somehow, as if he wasn't real. But he *was* real. She knew that now, and this time there was no going back. Somehow she had to warn him, had to try and save his life. Deep inside she shuddered, trying to remember the date on the gravestone. It jumped into her thoughts with startling clarity: August 30th 2010. Just four short weeks away.

If only she could talk to someone who would listen, someone who wouldn't whisk her straight off to see a doctor, or call her grandparents. Something inside her niggled, a fleeting memory that brought a tiny dash of hope, and she stopped, turning her bicycle around in the road and heading back the way she had come.

❀ ❀ ❀ ❀ ❀

It was a long haul to Brewster's farm, and by the time she
had pedaled up the final hill Cass's legs were aching. She
clambered off her bicycle, unsure now that she was actually
here. Maybe this wasn't such a good idea after all.

The farmer was letting the cows out after milking, and
she stood back in the hedge as they lumbered by. They
stared at her with huge brown eyes and mooed softly. The
dog behind them stopped for a moment, squirming up
against her, and she leaned down to stroke its matted coat,
glad of an excuse to stall.

"Here, Nell," bellowed the farmer, letting out a piercing
whistle, and the dog was off like a shot, following the
lumbering herd around the corner and out of sight. Cass
watched them go, breathing in the fresh scents of morning,
loneliness a heavy cloud that weighed her down as she turned
back the way she had come. What was she thinking, coming
here? Maybe they were right, and she really was crazy.

Mabel Bell loved to walk to the end of the road and watch
the cows wander by. There was a timelessness to their
gentle ambling that brought her sharply back in touch with
the reality that often seemed to evade her nowadays. Paul
always insisted that she shouldn't go out alone, but who
was he to tell her what to do? At seventy-two years old she
considered herself perfectly capable of deciding her own
actions. Or was she seventy three? Birthdays seemed to fly
by so quickly nowadays.

She watched the small, slightly built teenager stroking
old Nell and a pinprick of memory brought a heavy worry.
She had seen the girl before, she was sure of it, but where?
It came to her in a rare blinding flash of clarity; Tanya's
friend, the girl with the dream. Now what was her name?

She reached out her hand as the girl turned toward her, trying to remember.

"Hello," she called, her voice thin and reedy.

The girl turned back, a smile lighting up her drawn features. "Hello, Mrs. Bell, I was hoping to find you."

"Cassandra," murmured Mabel. That was it, the girl who had helped Tanya with Typhoon. She walked slowly toward her, the two black and white sheepdogs close at her heels, like shadows. They sank down onto their haunches when she stopped in front of Cass, pink tongues lolling from the sides of their mouths.

"Why do you want to see me?" she asked directly, a gentle smile playing on her lips.

"I…" Cass froze, unsure now of her decision. Mabel Bell had probably forgotten all about their last little chat by now. She stumbled on awkwardly, staring at her boots. "Do you remember the last time we spoke… I mean… about my dream?"

"Ah, yes … the cross-country," nodded the old lady.

A prickle of relief flooded Cass's senses. "Yes, yes," she cried, clasping her hands together. "And do you remember me telling you about M… Michael Miller, and his fall down the bank?"

"Sit down," suggested Mabel, lowering her frail form carefully onto a tree trunk that had lain in the side of road since last winter's storms. "And tell me all about it."

It was such a relief for Cass to have an understanding audience that she blurted out her story without pausing for breath. Mabel narrowed her eyes, trying to make sense of it, and then smiled. "Do you remember me telling you that things have a way of working themselves out?" she asked.

Cass nodded eagerly.

"Well, maybe that's just it," she went on slowly. "Maybe

this M, as you call him, has come to Hope Bank so that you can find a way to change his fate."

"But what if I can't?" cried Cass. "And should I try and warn him?"

Mabel sat for a moment, her hands crossed on her lap, then she looked up at Cass, carefully scrutinizing her face as if for answers. "No one can really tell you what to do," she went on, placing her hand against her heart. "It's in here, the truth, and all you can do is to try to find it."

"But why does no one else believe me?" sighed Cass.

Mabel smiled, reaching out a hand to stroke one of the dogs; it squirmed against her, rolling over onto its back. "Maybe I've just lived a lot longer and seen a lot more than most of the others you try to speak to. Maybe twenty years ago I too would have laughed at your fears... but now I know."

She looked up at Cass, holding her gaze for a moment, a powerful clarity in her faded blue eyes. "I am at the end of my life now. I can see things from a different place and I have come to realize that anything is possible. I believe your story and I also believe that you will find the right answers, but no one can tell you what to do. Follow your heart and your instincts, for the right path is there, hidden deep inside you. Fate is playing a game with you, and you just have to play along with it in your own way."

As Cass cycled toward Hope Bank again, half an hour later, her heart felt lighter than it had in weeks. She believed in herself now, and she finally had a purpose. All she could do was to wait for the right moment and then go with her gut instinct... It was the waiting that was going to be the hardest thing now.

CHAPTER 9

"Now then, Michael," grinned Robert Ashton, his silver head bright in the dim light of the barn. "How are you settling in so far?"

The young man looked over from where he was busily grooming Archie, a big chestnut youngster. He tapped his currycomb on the wall and grinned, one hand resting on the horse's gleaming rump. "I'm enjoying it so far. It's great to have so many different types of horses to work with."

"Well, you can give this fellow a little schooling if you like," suggested Robert. "When you've finished brushing him, of course. He's an awkward customer, remember, so stay focused and alert; he's only been backed a month and he's about ready to try cantering, but he likes to buck, so take it slowly."

Michael's eyes lit up, loving the thought of a challenge. "I'll do my best," he promised.

Cass immediately saw him as she rode her bicycle in through the entrance to Hope Bank – a glimpse was all she needed to recognize the young man who had been haunting her dreams. She stopped, one foot on the pedal, heart thudding heavily beneath her rib cage while her nerves did a crazy dance. He sat so tall yet loose and free, moving easily with every stride as the big chestnut horse beneath him extended across the school. Something inside her tightened, but how could she warn him? What could she say?

Mabel's voice came into her head. *"Fate is playing a game with you and you just have to follow your instincts and play it your own way."* But what was the way? With a heavy sigh she tore her eyes away from the straight-backed rider on the chestnut horse and headed off toward the stable yard.

"Cass, right?" he called after her. "I'm sorry that I had such a bad effect on you last time. Are you feeling better now?"

Cass's heart tightened; his voice was so deep and vibrant and alive… for now. She turned back to face him, a smile forced onto her tight lips. Every day she was living a lie, with her parents and with the Ashtons, but not with Mabel Bell and never with *him*, M; but how to tell him the truth? She had four short weeks to make him believe her story and she needed to tread very carefully so she wouldn't blow her chance to save him. "*Trust your instincts and play the game.*" She just had to wait for the right moment and that moment wasn't now.

"Hi," she cried. "Yes, I'm fine now. Thanks, Michael."

He grinned and her heart turned over. "Oh, you remember my name, huh?"

"Archie is doing well," she responded, changing the subject.

"He wasn't twenty minutes ago."

He trotted toward her, reining in at the fence, his eyes sparkling with merriment… and life. "He almost bucked me off when I tried to put him into canter."

"I saw your horse, he's nice. Does he jump?"

He rolled his eyes, nodding. "A little. He needs a lot more experience, though. I won't be bringing him to work with me every day, of course, but Robert said that he'd try to give me a hand with his jump training today, if there's time."

"I'm taking Ty – that's my horse – to the Ripton show soon. Will you be going there, do you think?"

Tired of standing still, the big chestnut, Archie, sidled

impatiently. Michael took up the reins, speaking to him in a soft undertone before looking back at Cass. "I guess so," he responded. "It's not very far from where I live, but, of course, I might be working. I'm only supposed to be part time here because I still have horses at home to take care of too, but I'm still not sure what days Robert wants me yet."

"Of course, he might want you to compete there with some of his youngsters," suggested Cass.

His eyes lit up. "Do you think so? That would be great!"

She shrugged. "Well, that's what Jack Donelly used to do, and you are kind of his replacement, I guess."

For a moment there was silence as their eyes met and moved away again. Cass felt the color rise in her face. "I suppose you live pretty close, then, if you're coming in every day, I mean?"

She delivered her question in what she hoped was a cool and casual tone, trying to ignore the erratic beating of her heart as she waited for his answer.

Sensing her discomfort, however, he flashed her a broad grin, leaning forward to run his hand down the big chestnut's damp neck. "Oh, you probably wouldn't know it, it's not so far away, but it's just a tiny place that no one ever seems to have heard of."

"I *might* know it," she responded, holding her breath.

He sat up tall in the saddle, looking her straight in the eye. "It's a place called Ridgeway Farm. Well that's where we actually live, although it's not really a farm anymore. The nearby village is called Hawk Ridge."

Hawk Ridge… Hawk Ridge… Hawk Ridge… The sign flashed into Cass's mind, there on the side of the lane, another piece of the puzzle slipping neatly into place, as if fate was laughing in her face. She couldn't play this game anymore; she would just have to tell him.

He was looking at her earnestly, a frown clouding his face. "Are you OK?"

"Yes…yes… I have to go, though," she mumbled, scurrying off across the yard with her heart beating so hard in her ears that she thought the whole world must surely hear it.

The young man from her dream – or premonition, if that was what it was – sat quite still on the gleaming chestnut horse, watching her hasty retreat with a curious expression in his dark eyes. What's bugging this gorgeous girl with amazing brown eyes, he wondered? One thing was for sure; he was determined to find out.

By half past two the chores were almost done; Michael walked into the tack room just as Cass and Laura were finishing off the last of the saddles.

"Robert has been called away, so he can't do my lesson today after all," he announced. "I thought that I might just take Tempest out for some exercise and I wondered if you girls wanted to come along and show me the best trails."

"Tempest?" remarked Laura. "That's a coincidence, Cass's horse is named Typhoon. Two storms in one stable, so to speak."

"We had a Typhoon once," he responded, frowning slightly. "We used to breed a little… before my dad died last year, all our Ridgeway horses were named after something to do with the weather. There was Snowstorm and Sunshine…"

He turned away suddenly, looking down at his boots and Cass stepped forward, automatically reaching out to touch his arm. "I'm sorry about your dad."

He looked back at her for a moment, meeting her gaze with a dark intensity before closing his hand briefly over hers. A warm tingle flooded her skin; he was so vibrant, so alive, how could –?

"Thanks," he murmured. "Now, how about it? Who's coming for a ride?"

By the time the two girls were tacked up and ready, Michael was riding his powerful gray around the outdoor ring. He raised a hand in greeting as he cantered by, slowing to a trot and heading toward the gate. Tempest whinnied a high-pitched cry of recognition and he reined in, an expression of amazement on his tanned face. "I don't believe it!" he cried.

"Don't believe what?" retorted Laura.

"When you told me that your horse was named Typhoon I didn't realize that he was *that* Typhoon."

Cass looked at him nervously. "What do you mean? What Typhoon?"

"We bred him," he cried. "Well, I mean my dad did. In fact, believe it or not, he and Tempest here are twins."

"That's crazy," giggled Laura.

For Cass it seemed inevitable. Another link that intertwined her whole existence with his; another sign to be noted and acted upon in this crazy game she was playing. A tingling sensation choked her throat and her hands on the reins turned clammy.

"I know," he agreed. "You're both thinking, how can a big powerful gray be twins with this little black fellow here. Well, twins aren't always identical, you know."

Laura was intrigued by his revelation. "But when did you sell him?" she asked. "And did you break him in?"

Michael nodded, a faraway look in his eyes for a moment. "Yes, I broke him in, well, at least Dad and I did. We sold him soon after, though."

"Why?" blurted out Cass. "Why did you keep Tempest and sell Typhoon?"

"I didn't want to, I always felt that there was more to him than Dad gave him credit for. But he was just so nervy and spooky and we didn't think he had the temperament to make it as a show jumper – or at least Dad didn't. Anyway, I'm glad he's found a good home. I loved the little guy, but my dad..."

He hesitated, urging Tempest out into the road, as if afraid of saying too much.

"Your dad what?" demanded Cass, riding alongside him. The two horses sidled together in silent greeting, prancing with excitement as she waited for his answer.

"He believed that there was something strange about him, that's all."

"What kind of strange?" insisted Cass.

He shrugged awkwardly, catching her eye and then glancing away again. "He thought that Ty could see things that others couldn't, and that was why he was so crazy."

"Well maybe he can," replied Cass thoughtfully, her heart pounding with possibilities.

They were out for just half an hour, during which time Laura and Michael seemed to have pushed all comments about Typhoon to the back of their minds. It was only Cass who felt the impact of his revelation and realized its importance. It filled her head as she rode along the road behind the other two horses, taking over her every thought, even when they galloped off ahead of her, away across the pasture. Michael looked back at her, his dark eyes sparkling. "Come on," he called.

Typhoon half reared, snorting, while images still flashed in front of her like pictures in a movie show; Typhoon

as a foal and yearling, staring into the distance, seeing…
what? If, as Mabel Bell believed, fate really was playing a
game with her, then she had to think of this as just another
clue, another piece of the puzzle that she needed to solve if
she was to save him from his doom. *Him,* Michael Miller,
M, the young man from her dream, the young man who
was here right now, so alive and full of hope. A wave of
fear swelled inside her. What if she failed, if she couldn't
save him after all? The answer came at once; she would
just have to find another way to change his fate; or maybe
fate was inevitable and there *was* no way to save him. A
shudder passed through her at the thought.

The figures up ahead of her were a blur now. She blinked
hard to try and regain her focus as Typhoon bunched himself
beneath her, lunging forward with a surge of power, taking
hold of the bridle with little resistance from his rider; ears
flat against his skull as he leaped into a gallop. Strangely
distanced from the world around her, Cass just let him go; if
fate wanted to play games with her, then get on with it. And
what happened then? Would she die too, here on this stark
hillside? Was she destined to fall down the incline, just like
the Michael Miller in her dream?

Typhoon threw himself against the bridle, faltering
slightly when he felt no pull on the reins, slithering to a halt
behind the other two horses with an air of disappointment
at being unable to frighten his rider.

"Wow," cried Michael, cheeks glowing and dark eyes
alight with elation. "That was awesome."

Cass just looked at him, her eyes huge against the pallor
of her skin. She would have to tell him, there was nothing
else to do. She would find the right moment and just tell him
what had happened on cross-country day. There, the next
piece of the puzzle was laid; she just had to slot it into place.

❀ ❀ ❀ ❀ ❀

Cass was concerned that Laura might think that her friend was behaving strangely as they trotted homeward, but if she did she kept her observations to herself. Maybe she's just glad to have Michael's undivided attention, thought Cass.

Occasionally Michael glanced back curiously, trying to catch her eye, but she ignored him, staying focused and feeling much better now that she had a plan – even though her heart was beating so hard that it felt as if it was about to jump right out of her chest.

She would wait until he had un-tacked, she decided, and find a moment to get him alone. Words whirled around inside her head. What to say, though… how to start…?

The moment came as naturally as breathing.

Flushed from sweeping the yard, Cass stopped for a moment, leaning on her broom, watching the dappled sunlight make flickering, magical patterns on the ground. Laura had gone into town with her mother and old Silas was in the far meadow so only she and Michael were left in the yard. She could hear him whistling softly from the barn where he was busy filling hay nets. Was this the moment? Should she just walk in there now and tell him, "Don't ride out on the 30th of August"?

The cry that came from the barn, breaking the calm silence of the afternoon, shattered her thoughts into a million tiny pieces and suddenly she was running toward it with everything else swept from her mind. She was almost at the half-open door when it suddenly burst open and for half a second she was faced by a small chestnut whirlwind. The inevitable thud as Bobby's head hit her full in the stomach seemed to happen in slow motion, knocking the wind out of

her, and then the ground came up to meet her, hard and solid.
As she waited for the pain to come she heard the sound of
unshod hooves, galloping off across the yard and then came
a voice, cutting through its first powerful wave.

"Cass, are you all right?"

Michael's worried voice filled her head as she struggled
for breath. His arm came about her shoulders, firm yet
gentle. "Yes," she gasped. "I-I think so."

He carried her easily into the barn, laying her gently
down onto the hay he had shaken out for the nets. "There
was this chestnut Shetland," he groaned. "I tried to grab it
and it gave me both back feet."

"Bobby," she croaked, fighting off the pain that had
settled into a dull ache across her chest.

"You don't think anything is broken, do you?" cried
Michael and she managed a weak smile.

"Just my pride."

"And your stomach, I bet," he responded, placing a
gentle hand on the sorest place.

She sat up awkwardly with a sudden rush of
embarrassment, gasping as a sharp pain shot through
her head. "Bobby is a pain in the neck, I'm afraid," she
told him. "He's as old as the hills, but Robert adores him
because he's had him since he was a boy and the little
monster can do no wrong in his eyes, even though he's
always causing trouble."

Wincing, she clambered up to sit down beside Michael,
who had perched himself on a hay bale. "Someone should
have warned you about him," she remarked.

"Should I go and try to catch him?" he asked, but she
shook her head.

"No, Bobby gets to do pretty much whatever he wants
around here. He'll be fine. Did he actually kick you?"

117

"He sure did," groaned Michael, rubbing his thigh and suddenly they were both laughing hysterically.

It was Cass who regained control first. Wiping her eyes, she looked up at M, suddenly serious. "I saw you before you came here," she said, amazed at her own words.

"Saw me where?" he responded.

"Well, that's just it." She looked at her hands, splaying out her fingers. "I know this sounds stupid, but it was in a kind of dream."

"A dream?" he echoed.

"Yes, a dream," she went on, suddenly determined to say her piece. "The first time that I ever rode Ty he galloped off with me in the cross-country, and I had a kind of weird dream – they say that I fell and hit my head, but I know that I didn't."

"And that was when you saw me?"

"Yes." She looked up at him, chewing her bottom lip as she searched for the right words. "Something frightened your horse and he fell down a bank at the side of the road. You –"

"I what?" butted in Michael.

"You were hurt," she finished lamely.

"And you thought that it was some kind of premonition and you are trying to warn me?"

"Something like that."

"But how do you know when it was – or is – to be?"

Cass froze. How could she tell him that she saw his gravestone?

"If I don't know when then how can I prepare?" he asked earnestly, the flicker of a smile behind his eyes.

"I'm telling the truth," she insisted, annoyed. "And if you don't believe me then you'll be the one who'll suffer."

Reaching out to place a hand on her arm he smiled

apologetically. "Look, I'm sorry, I know that you mean well, but you must admit it does sound pretty crazy."

"Suit yourself," she responded, standing up abruptly. A wave of pain across her rib cage forced her back down again. "And it was August 30th, if you're interested."

"Look," the expression of concern on his face made her feel a bit better. "If I promise to take good care of myself on August 30th, then will you forgive me for not believing that you can see into the future?"

For just a moment she held his dark eyes with hers, eyes that sparkled with merriment. He was just humoring her, she could see that, and she didn't really blame him; after all, what would she have thought if someone came up to her with such a crazy story?

"This has never happened to me before," she told him.

"You've probably never had such a bad fall before," he responded.

"It wasn't the fall," she began. "It was –"

"Hi guys!" announced Laura from the doorway. "Having fun?"

"I met Bobby," groaned Michael. "First he got me with both back hooves and then he nearly knocked poor Cass here to kingdom come. I think she hit her head too."

So that's it, thought Cass hopelessly. He believed that she was just rambling on after getting hit on the head; it was just like the last time. Closing her eyes for just a second she saw the image of him falling down the bank. He and Tempest, rolling over and over, entwined together, and the awkwardly slumped shape of him when everything became still again… the silence.

"What are your grandparents going to say when we take you home with a bang on the head yet again?" groaned Laura.

"Nothing," announced Cass. "Because I'm not going home yet and we are definitely not going to tell them. Anyway, I didn't bang my head."

"That's what she said the last time," Laura remarked to M, raising her eyebrows.

He nodded, giving Cass's shoulder a brief, sympathetic squeeze. "Well, you seem okay now, so why don't we just forget about it?" he suggested.

She felt his fingers through her sweater, warm and firm and so, so alive. Oh, how could she make him believe her? How could she warn him that he might only have a few short weeks to live? Yet again the thought came into her mind, but what if there was no way to change fate? What if it had been a glimpse of the inevitable?

CHAPTER 10

Typhoon shivered, steadying his legs and shaking the water from his coat, a million tiny droplets sparkling in the afternoon sunshine.

"Hey, watch it," cried Michael, cowering back from the spray.

Cass couldn't help but giggle. "Sorry," she eventually managed, scrambling for the hose that had fallen from her hand. It slithered like a yellow serpent across the ground, frightening Ty, who spun around in a circle, knocking her sideways and releasing a jet of water that suddenly took on a life of its own.

Michael made a grab for the writhing hose while Cass hung onto Typhoon's lead rope. "He'll never let me bathe him again," she groaned.

He grinned, regained control of the offending object and turned down the pressure. "It might help if you didn't have it on so high," he remarked. "Come on, I'll give you a hand."

After half an hour of struggling, Typhoon was finally done. He raised his top lip in disgust, gleaming from head to toe. "You'd better walk him to dry him off," Michael suggested. "Oh, and by the way –"

"By the way what?"

Cass looked around eagerly, catching the amused glint in his eyes. "It's August 27th so isn't it about time that you gave me another of your lectures about being careful on the 30th, or has your head cleared?"

She turned back toward Typhoon, shrugging off her annoyance as she urged him to walk on. "My head's always clear," she retorted.

"Well, that's good," he laughed. "I don't need to worry any more, then."

It had been a strange few weeks, she reflected fifteen minutes later as she let the black gelding nibble some grass on the shoulder of the road near the entrance to Hope Bank. M (he was always M in her head) believed that she was slightly crazy, she was sure of that, for she had tried on more than one occasion to warn him about August 30th. She should have saved her breath though, she reflected, for he thought the whole thing was just a huge joke.

She had even tried to persuade him not to ride out on the roads for a while, but he had simply laughed at that suggestion. "I need to go along the road when I take the horses out for exercise at home," he had insisted. "It's the only way to get to the bridle path onto the pastures. Anyway, you'll see, I'm going to prove to you once and for all that you're talking a load of nonsense. On August 31st you'll be apologizing to me, you'll see."

She remembered that they had been in the tack room at the time, carefully soaping their tack. The sweet smell of leather filled the air with its distinctive aroma, and dust had danced in a beam of sunshine as M caught her eye, his expression strangely serious for once.

"You just can't let yourself believe stuff like that, Cass," he had told her. "Think of it like this; if I listened to you now, what would it be next? Death threats, ghostly horses in the night? You have to get a grip on yourself."

After that remark Cass hadn't dared to mention it again, but the worry of it still hung like a heavy weight around her shoulders, coloring her every waking moment. A couple of days ago, in desperation, she had even decided to try and

123

talk to Mabel Bell again – to Cass, the old lady was the only person who made any sense. To her dismay, however, Tanya had come into the yard the very next morning and asked her if she would mind taking over total care of Sunny for a while as she, her dad and her grandmother were going away on a two weeks' vacation.

"I'm sorry it's such short notice," she had apologized, "but Gran has been so out of sorts lately and Dad thought that it might do her good. He booked a trip to Europe just last night. It's always been her dream to see Venice."

Cass had smiled automatically, nodding her agreement and waving her off while inside it felt as if a door was slamming shut in her face; never in her whole life had she felt so alone.

"You don't think I'm crazy, do you?" she murmured to Typhoon, wondering if the horrors of cross-country day were just as fresh in his mind. He lifted his head, snorted loudly and dropped his nose to the ground again, eagerly cropping the fresh green grass as if he didn't have a care in the world. Cass listened to the rhythmic sound of his chewing with a hopeless sigh, watching the sun make dappled patterns on the ground as she tried to turn her thoughts to something else, like tomorrow and the Ripton show, for instance.

Her heart quickened as she realized that the day she had been dreaming of for so long was almost here. Maybe she should just forget about her stupid premonition. After all, everyone else thought she was crazy, and maybe they were right. She pulled Typhoon's head up from the grass determinedly, and led him back toward the stable yard. From now on, she decided, she would let nature take its course and just concentrate on tomorrow and nothing else.

❀ ❀ ❀ ❀ ❀

In an effort to take her mind of her ever-present worries, Cass biked over to Tall Trees to see Anna and Duke after she'd finished her chores for the day.

To her surprise the plump gray cob was still in his stable, eagerly munching on a hay net and totally drowned by a voluminous lilac cotton sheet.

"Guess where we're going tomorrow?" cried Anna, appearing suddenly from the tack room with a gleaming saddle over her arm.

Cass shrugged. "Where? Where are you going?"

"Guess!" insisted Anna, twirling around in a circle. "Come on, guess where we're going."

"I don't know," laughed Cass. "You tell me."

"The Ripton show," exclaimed Anna, unable to contain her excitement. "Duke and I, we're going to the Ripton show and I'm entered in the equitation class. I was going to surprise you, but now that you're here –"

"That's fantastic, Anna," cried Cass, genuinely happy for her friend. "I knew that you two were doing well, but I didn't realize that you were that confident."

"And it's all because of you," mumbled Anna awkwardly. "Duke would probably have been sold by now if you hadn't helped me with him."

"Well, I wouldn't go so far as to say that," responded Cass. "Anyway, come on, tell me what classes you're going to enter."

Half an hour later, as Cass biked slowly home, for the first time in ages she felt a warm glow inside her. She just felt so excited for Anna – and a little proud of herself too. Maybe all her fears for M *were* just a crazy dream after all; maybe she should just concentrate on the show and stop her stupid worrying. Three more days, that's all there was anyway.

125

Tomorrow was the 28th – the day of the show, which would take her mind totally off it. Then after that all she had to do was get through the 29th and the 30th and it would all be over. Michael's face flashed into her mind; the humor in his dark eyes, and the way his teeth shone white against his tanned skin when he laughed. He was just so alive. Surely there was no way that... that...

She stood up, increasing the pressure on the pedals and pumping her legs up and down so hard that her muscles screamed with agony, anything to chase away her fears, the fears that lurked behind her like a pack of prowling wolves.

Tomorrow was all that mattered now, Typhoon's chance for glory – the culmination of all her dreams and *her* chance to prove to everyone that the beautiful black horse was worthy of the confidence she had placed in him.

And M? Her heart quickened. Fate was just going to have to run its course. After all, there was nothing else could she do now, short of tying him down.

CHAPTER 11

A single beam of light cast through Cass's bedroom window. She watched its silvery gleam, the breath catching in her throat as reality banished her dreams. This was it, today, the Ripton show.

All thoughts of sleep cast aside, she leaped from her bed and raced to the window to greet the first glimmer of dawn. They were setting off at seven, and she wanted to braid Typhoon's mane first, since he was sure to have slept in the dirtiest part of his stable. She scrambled eagerly into her best cream-colored jodhpurs, pulling on a pair of jeans over them to keep them clean before running her fingers through her hair and splashing her face with water.

To her surprise, when she burst into the kitchen her grandmother was already there, rubbing her bleary eyes as she packed sandwiches into a plastic box. "I didn't think you'd feel like any breakfast, so take these for later, love," she said, handing them to her.

Cass gave her an appreciative hug, her heart racing at the prospect of the day to come. "Will you and Granddad be able to come and watch?" she asked, suddenly needing the support.

"We'll do our best," promised Sarah Truman, pushing a stray lock of gray hair back behind her ears. "You just go and enjoy yourself." For a moment a shadow clouded her lined face. "And you will be careful, won't you?"

"Don't worry," Cass grinned, reassuring her. "Typhoon is very sensible now, you'll see. Today he's going to prove everyone wrong."

"Well, good luck."

As she climbed onto her ancient bicycle, Cass glanced back again, toward her grandmother, who was now standing in the open doorway, her arms clasped around herself.

"Honestly, Gran, you really don't need to worry about me," she insisted.

"I'll always worry," smiled Sarah Truman. "That's what parents and grandparents do. They would have been so proud of you, you know."

"I know," smiled Cass, holding her gaze for a second, and then she was off down the road, her whole mind tuned into the events of the day ahead.

By the time she arrived at Hope Bank the yard was already abuzz. "Call this an early start?" cried Robert Ashton as she deposited her bicycle against the wall. "We'll be loading up soon."

"Ignore him," joined in Laura. "He just appeared himself."

"Well, I was first here," grumbled Silas, trundling by with a heaped wheelbarrow, "and I'm not even going to the show."

Cass smiled at him, glancing eagerly around the yard. "You're always first, though, Silas. Isn't Michael here yet?"

"Ah-ha, missing the new boy already, eh, Cass?" teased Robert.

Cass flushed. "Of course I'm not," she retorted crossly. "I just wondered, that's all."

"Don't listen to my dad," smiled Laura. "Michael's going to the show straight from home, since it's just down the road from his house. He's taking his own two horses anyway, as well as riding for us. Oh, and guess what?"

Cass stopped and looked into her friend's glowing face. "What?"

"Dad's going to let me take the jumping pony he just bought into the junior jumping class."

"What new jumping pony?" frowned Cass. "I didn't see it yesterday."

"That," announced Laura, "is because we haven't even gotten it home yet. We're picking it up at the show today."

"Will you two girls stop chatting and get the horses ready," roared Robert. "Or no one will be going to the show today."

Forty-five minutes later the Ashtons' silver trailer rumbled out of the yard, swaying slightly as its precious cargo of horses stamped restlessly, trying to find their balance.

"I wish Mom had been able to come today," grumbled Laura.

Robert Ashton glanced at his daughter before turning his attention back to the road. "She's got a lot going on at the moment, and she wanted to catch up on some paperwork, but she might turn up at lunch time."

"With some sandwiches, I hope."

Robert grinned. "That's what I'm counting on."

Cass took in their cheerful banter, wishing that she could feel as relaxed; for the Ashtons this might be just another day at another show, but to her it was a milestone. What if Typhoon went crazy again? What if, what if, what if? So many what ifs. She put them firmly out of her head. *What if M dies on Monday?*

A cold trickle rippled down her spine. No, not now, she wasn't going to let this spoil her day. She wasn't even going to let herself think about that today.

"You okay, Cass?"

Laura's eyes were narrowed, a concerned frown marking the smooth sweep of her brow.

Cass jumped, forcing a smile onto her face and turning

her attention to the blurred hedge beyond the window. "Yes, of course. Thanks."

"She's just a bit nervous, aren't you?" remarked Robert.

Cass nodded. "Uh... yeah, a little, I guess. I'll just go and check on Ty."

The showground was already buzzing with life when the Ashtons' trailer rolled in through the gate, lurching across the grass to the very end of a long row of vehicles.

"There's Michael's truck," shrieked Laura.

They could see him just a little further down, already mounted on a slim chestnut.

"That must be the four-year-old he was telling us about," Laura went on eagerly. "What was its name?"

"Something dumb, if I remember correctly," retorted her dad, cutting the engine.

"Marmalade," responded Cass. "He named it Marmalade."

"Well, it will probably be in your class, Cass," Laura reminded her.

Cass grinned, suddenly getting things into better perspective. "It makes no difference to me who's in our class. If we just get around I'll be happy."

She reflected upon that comment as she rode Typhoon around the busy showground a short time later. The black gelding felt as if he was wired, his whole body taut with an explosive excitement that threatened to burst out at any moment. She tried to relax, keeping her reins as loose as she dared and her legs light on his heaving sides. To even get him into the ring seemed totally hopeless at the moment, let alone take him over any fences; there was just too much going on, too much bustle and excitement.

For a fleeting moment she spotted Laura in the collecting ring, warming up for the open jumping class. Steel appeared totally composed, bored almost, by the electric atmosphere, and ignored the jostle of horses around him, his mind securely fixed on the practice fence as his tall, slightly built rider turned him toward it. Typhoon sidled, champing on the bit, and Cass closed her hand on the reins. Would he ever be like that, she wondered, watching Steel spring into the air and land in effortless slow motion on the other side of the fence.

A movement from nearby took her attention, a flash of color and an excited cry. A boy appeared suddenly in front of them, a small boy with golden curls and an impish grin, proudly waving a bright red balloon. For one frozen moment Cass's heart fell. Typhoon snorted, running backwards, and with two huge, unseating leaps, he was off. Her head roared as she fought for control, but then suddenly something was there, blocking her panicked horse's flight.

"Taking off on another one of your crazy gallops?" remarked a familiar voice.

Typhoon slithered to a halt, snorting, and Cass gathered up the reins, regaining the delicate strands of control.

"It was that stupid balloon," she cried, looking up into M's sparkling eyes, her cheeks burning. "It spooked him."

"Good thing I was around to stop him," he remarked. "You may have gotten to see into my future again, and who knows what you would have come across this time."

Cass tried to thank him but her words came out jumbled and mismatched. He raised his hand. "Look," he suggested. "Your class isn't for almost an hour yet. Why don't you let me try and help you calm your lunatic horse down before

131

he kills you? Hey, now there's a thought. Maybe all your talk about seeing me fall was really about you? Maybe *I* just changed *your* fate by stopping Ty from bolting off."

Cass found her voice. "Who knows," she mumbled, her confidence growing. "And anyway, how can you help me to get him to calm down?"

"Well, you can already see how fickle fate is," went on Michael with laughter in his eyes, "so I think that it's time you stopped worrying about what might be and get on with what's happening now. All we have to do is find a quiet corner and let Typhoon get used to the atmosphere from a short distance. You're expecting too much of him, you know. No youngster goes to its first show or two without getting a bit spooked, and your crazy horse is already totally spooked before he even starts."

Cass stared hard at Typhoon's neat braids, fumbling with her reins. "Do you think…" The flush spread down her neck. "I mean… will you come with me?"

"Course I will," he grinned, his teeth flashing white. "For a while anyway, and then we'll go over to the practice ring."

As they rode together across the busy showground, Typhoon sidling close to Michael's chestnut for support, Cass felt a bubble of happiness gurgle inside her. He even knew when her class was and he had offered to help her. She glanced up, catching his eye and seeing… No, she decided, pushing the images aside. M was right; she wasn't going to even think about the day after tomorrow again. Today was what counted, *today,* when she was going to jump a clear round and prove everyone wrong about Typhoon.

"You can do it, Cass," murmured Michael, almost as if reading her thoughts. She nodded imperceptibly. "I can," she responded almost silently.

133

❀ ❀ ❀ ❀ ❀

True to his word, Michael worked his magic on Typhoon; within half an hour he had the nervous black gelding and his equally nervous rider clearing the practice fence like old hands. Cass looked out for him as she cantered out of the competition ring fifteen minutes later, a broad smile plastered across her face

Typhoon bucked beneath her, a huge explosive eruption of pure pleasure, and she leaned forward to pat his neck, her eyes glowing as she looked across and caught Michael's eye. "I told you that you could do it," he called, hurrying toward her.

"Well done, beautiful clear round," boomed Robert Ashton's familiar voice as she slipped to the ground on legs like jelly.

She passed the reins over Ty's head, leaning against his shoulder for support. "It was thanks to Michael, really," she admitted. "He helped me to calm him down. Well, calm us both down, to be totally honest."

Robert nodded. "Thank heavens for that. I was a little worried about you, but Laura's class was already starting as we arrived."

"How did she do?"

"Second," replied Robert, rolling his eyes. "She's gone over to the junior ring now with the new pony, so I suppose I'd better get going and see what they're up to."

"Second!" cried Cass as he turned away. "That's great, isn't it?"

He glanced back, shaking his silvery head. "Only first is good enough for Hope Bank stables, except for you, of course. You got a nice clear round, now go for another. But do NOT try anything stupid like going against the clock."

"You really will ruin him if you start trying to go too

fast too soon," agreed Michael. "Anyway, I'd better take off too and work your colored horse in, Robert. His class is next."

A surge of guilt turned Cass's mouth dry. She had spent all this time with M, even riding over to the trailer with him when he went to put Marmalade away, and she hadn't even thought to ask him how *he* had done so far.

She opened her mouth to pose the question but Robert was already asking it. "How did *you* do, Mike? You haven't told us that."

Michael just grinned, already walking off. "First," he called back.

"Well, make sure that you ride my horse just as well," Robert responded. "He hasn't even managed to get a clear round this season, to be totally honest."

Michael hesitated for a moment, running his hand through his thatch of dark hair. "I'll do my best," he promised, "but I can't work miracles."

Miracles, thought Cass. Did they really happen? M had insisted that fate was just a fickle strand of chance that changed continuously and that he had changed *her* fate today, by stopping Typhoon. So had his own fate changed, then? Oh, how she hoped so.

By the time they were called in for the jump-off Cass could feel a change in Typhoon. Instead of feeling slightly explosive beneath her his feet seemed almost to drag, and he hit the first fence hard with both front feet. The pole fell with a heavy thud and he kicked his heels in objection, proceeding to clear all the other fences with ease.

"That was great, Cass," called Robert, who had come back with Laura from the junior jumping ring especially to watch. "He's tired, that's all; it takes a lot out of a young horse you know, all that excitement and adrenalin."

Cass nodded, concealing her slight prickle of disappointment. "Thanks."

"You would have been happy with one clear round this morning," Laura reminded her.

"You're right," agreed Cass, patting Typhoon's damp neck. "A whole lot more than happy, really. So how did the new pony do?"

Laura and her father exchanged a glance. "First," he announced proudly.

"Its price just doubled then, I guess," laughed Cass.

"And so will Typhoon's, I would imagine," joined in a high-pitched, reedy voice.

"Grandma?" shrieked Cass, looking around to see both her grandparents standing nearby, looking slightly uncomfortable in the unfamiliar surroundings. "You saw him jump?"

"Of course we did," they responded in unison.

"But we just thought that we'd stay out of your way until you were finished," added Sarah Truman.

Her husband was beaming from ear to ear. "So, will you be selling him now that he's finally proved he's not a total lunatic?" he asked.

"Granddad!" cried Cass, "how could you even think of that? Typhoon will never be for sale."

"Everything has its price," remarked Robert Ashton, bobbing his silvery head up and down.

"Not in my world," announced Cass. "Come on, you two. Since you're here you might as well help me get loaded up."

"Glad to be of service," smiled Bill Truman, falling into step beside his granddaughter while the gleaming black

136

gelding followed behind them on a loose rein, snorting softly, completely at ease now with his surroundings.

"So when is your next show?" he asked eagerly.

As the silver truck carried its tired cargo homewards later that afternoon, Cass decided that, all in all, it *had* been a pretty amazing day.

On the way to the show she had spent most of the journey in the back, trying to calm Typhoon down, but now he was contentedly nibbling his hay net like an old campaigner, so she sat in the window seat, her eyelids drooping as the excitement of the day caught up with her.

The world passed by in a blur of color, ten thousand different shades of green spread across the hillside toward the horizon where oak and ash and silver birch met the clear bright blue of the summer sky, a row of neat white houses, and a solemn gray church.

"This is where Michael lives," announced Robert from the driver's seat.

Cass's eyes snapped wide open and she peered from the window, suddenly breathless. "Here?"

"Well, somewhere near here," responded Robert.

The glory of the day faded into oblivion and a cold clamminess brought a shiver to her limbs. There was the wide grass shoulder where she had seen the sign... and the steep bank beside the lane where...

The prowling wolves were snapping at her heels again. It was real; this place was real so it couldn't all have been just a dream. And suddenly there was the sign, looming before her: "HAWK RIDGE."

The place of nightmares.

"Are you okay?"

Laura's distant voice kicked into Cass's subconscious.

No…! No, she wasn't okay, for now she knew. M really *did* have just one more day before…

Her reply came out automatically while her heart beat so loudly that she could no longer hear herself think. "Yes, thanks… I'm just tired, that's all."

CHAPTER 12

What do you do when you know that something really bad is going to happen, but no one will believe you?

Cass tossed and turned in bed, her whole body damp with perspiration. How could she have believed it to be over; how could she not have trusted her intuition? She had just one day, one more day to try and persuade Michael to stay away from the road near his house. She knew full well what his response would be if she tried to talk to him again, though; he would give her that charming, disarming smile and scoff at her fears, and then probably deliberately ride along there just to prove his point.

Fate is just a fickle strand that can be broken in a moment, the path before you altered in the flicker of an eye. Was that true? She turned the thought around and around inside her head, hope flinging a lifeline. Maybe M's path had already been altered, maybe he was right all along, and the horror of cross-country day was just something that might have been if...

Sweat beaded on Cass's brow as the memories overloaded her imagination, fresh and terrifyingly real. She leaped from her bed, almost falling in her haste, hanging onto a chair for support as she scrambled into her clothes. It was no good just *hoping* that M's fate had changed; somehow she had to try to make sure that it had.

The idea came to her as she headed for Hope Bank, jogging on leaden legs since her bike had a punctured tire. She would go to Hawk Ridge today – the day before the 30th.

She would talk to Michael again and somehow make sure that nothing happened to him tomorrow.

For a moment she slowed her pace, looking around. Everything was fresh from the first shower of rain in a week. The scents, the early morning sounds, all were oozing with life. The image of Michael's face as his terrified gray horse plunged down the bank came into her head again; of Michael's face when he laughed, his dark eyes crinkling at the corners. Fear washed over her in an icy wave. There had to be a way to save him, there just had to be, and at least by riding over to his home she would be doing something. Maybe she could even try to talk to his mother. Then again, what would she say? One thing was sure in her mind though: she had to try.

If she really was to ride all the way to Hawk Ridge and back in daylight, Cass was well aware that she needed to set off as soon as possible, but what was she going to tell Laura and Robert? They would want to know why she was taking off on Ty before all the chores were finished. As it happened, fate herself lent a hand in that department. Maybe she really was just playing with everyone's lives, thought Cass, because just then Robert Ashton broke the sad news that was to pave the way for her departure.

Metal hooves sounded on concrete as a horse clattered into the yard and Cass looked up to see Robert jump down from the black Thoroughbred stallion, Marius.

"Silas," he roared, throwing the reins to Laura.

She grabbed them, frowning. "What's up, Dad?"

Cass rested her heavy wheelbarrow down onto the yard, her stomach churning at the expression on his drawn gray features. "What happened?" she cried.

Robert ran the back of his hand across his brow, his voice flat and empty. "It's Bobby," he groaned.

"What has the little monster done now?" smiled Laura.

Her father's face puckered and he dropped his head into his hands, his voice muffled as he tried to control his emotion. "He's... he's dead," he groaned. "Bobby is dead... in the far meadow."

"But how?" cut in Silas's shocked voice. He removed his cap, repeatedly sliding it on and off his head. "He was as fit as a fiddle yesterday."

"I'll get Mom," offered Laura, handing the stallion's reins to Cass.

Mollie Ashton's calm, sensible presence seemed to bring everything into perspective. "He was old, hon," she murmured to her grief-stricken husband. "And his heart probably just gave out. You should think of it as a godsend, really. He hasn't suffered and he died peacefully, here, at home."

Robert covered his wife's plump fingers with a broad tanned hand. "You're right, hon," he murmured. "I know that. It just seems like the end of an era."

"It won't be the same around the yard without his antics to put up with," announced Silas, rolling up his cap now and twisting it around and around.

"You can say that again," remarked Laura, and her father managed a weak smile.

"Okay, then," announced Mollie. "You two guys go off and see to him and I'll – see to the details," finished her mother awkwardly.

"I'll just put Marius away and give out the feeds, but then, well, I'm really sorry, but I'm afraid that I have to leave," announced Cass.

No one questioned her, no one told her that first she

141

must do this or that. No one cared in that instant about the jobs around the yard. As long as the horses were fed and happy, then the rest could wait.

As she rode along the lane a short time later Cass felt suddenly guilty at using poor old Bobby's death to her advantage. He had been an awkward pain in the neck most of the time, but they were all fond of him. Poor Robert must be devastated.

Grief twisted like a knife in her guts as the reality of it suddenly hit her. She would never see the bold little chestnut charging around the yard again, never try to hold him down for the dentist or the vet. A smile came from nowhere. She too had loved the old pony, but death comes to us all eventually and, as Mollie had said, he was very old and it was just his time. Unlike Michael.

Urging Typhoon into a trot, she stared toward the horizon. Oh, what was she doing here? What did she really think she could gain by going to Hawk Ridge today? Maybe she should just have ridden over there tomorrow, on the 30th, and just stayed all day to try and keep M off the lane. He wasn't going in to Hope Bank today, though, she remembered, so maybe she could catch him at home and just plead with him to listen. Yes, that was it, and even if he finally ended up believing that she really was crazy, then at least he might still be persuaded to keep his horses at home tomorrow.

The road ahead glistened dark gray and car tires swished through fresh puddles of water, making Typhoon spook. Cass hadn't actually given much thought to the fact that she was going to have to ride along the main road, so eager was she to get to Hawk Ridge, and now doubts set in again. Could she really do it? Could she actually ride all that way? A truck sounded its horn and Ty leaped sideways onto the shoulder, almost unseating her. She had to do it for Michael's sake, she told herself, concentrating on the clatter of hooves on the tarmac. "We can do it, we can do it, we can do it," she murmured in time with their rhythm, trying to force her thoughts back to yesterday's glory. *If you are feeling nervous or worried then try to concentrate on something good that has happened in your life,* her grandmother always told her.

Spooked by the traffic, Typhoon became more and more difficult to handle, trembling and prancing, his ears flickering back and forth. Cass had never been more relieved than when she turned off the busy main road, but the further she rode along the quiet, leafy road the more she began to question herself. Was this really the right way? After all, she had seen nothing of the cross-country course from where it all began in the first place. Maybe she had taken a totally wrong turn and this whole journey was a waste. Reining in, she took stock of her surroundings. There was the church they had passed yesterday. Wasn't it? Or did that church have a taller steeple?

Calmer now that they had left the buzz of vehicles behind, Ty lunged down for grass, and for a moment she allowed him to graze. Desolation stifled her, tightening her chest. What if, what if, what if? Was life just made up of what ifs? What if Michael Miller died tomorrow? She had to go on, there was nothing else to do!

When the sign for Hawk Ridge loomed at last, solid and real, her initial flood of relief was immediately overtaken by dread as she realized anew that this place really *had*

never been a dream, and that meant that her vision had been real, too. She pushed the thoughts to the very back of her mind, concentrating on the present. At least now she knew that she had come the right way, but where to go next?

Ahead of her the road narrowed and she reined in. Ty trembled beneath her, raising his head, ears pricked and muscles bunched, as if he could see more than she, as if he remembered. Deep inside, she shuddered. There was the place where the bank plunged steeply down, falling away from the side of the road to the place where... Oh, what was she doing here anyway? Suddenly all she wanted was to be back at home, safe at Hope Bank in Typhoon's own stable.

"Tell me, Ty,'" she pleaded. "Tell me what to do," but the black horse had his own agenda. He spun around in the road, quivering; white lather streaming down his neck as a rumbling sound filled Cass's ears. Too late she urged him onward, trying to find space as a huge truck roared into view, towering above them. For just a moment she saw the horror on the driver's white face. He hauled on the wheel, his brakes screaming... or was it her own voice Cass could hear? Something snapped inside her, some ridiculous realization. Was this *her* destiny, instead? Was it never meant for Michael? Or had fate just changed the game again?

Typhoon bunched himself beneath her, beyond all control. A roaring sound filled her head as he leaped into a gallop, and together they plunged down the bank, over and over, around and around, pain a huge weight, holding her down, dragging her into the darkness.

CHAPTER 13

The light that filtered into Cass's subconscious brought with it a vague sense of familiarity. This place where she had been before, this place where pain wracked her whole body and brought an icy cold fear into every recess of her being, took her straight back into her very worst nightmare. Michael! His name filled her head. She tried to speak, but no words came out, and then a cool hand on her brow brought back a semblance of sanity. A fall, she'd had a fall… his fall… but she wasn't dead… was she?

"Typhoon," she groaned, trying to force herself awake.

"Shush now, love, just sleep."

At the sound of her grandmother's voice Cass let out a whispering sigh. She was six years old again, hallucinating in the dark hours of a December night, the night after… after her parents died. The hollow emptiness echoed again inside her chest, loneliness a suffocating wave that slowly evaporated before the soothing touch of her grandmother's hand, allowing the comforting folds of sleep to ease her jarring pain.

When she woke again there were other sounds. Now, instantly, she knew where she was. "Michael," she groaned, remembering. What day was this, what time?

Her grandmother was still there. As she eased open her burning eyes Cass could see her rounded figure sitting beside the bed. Her eyes were half-closed but they snapped wide open when her granddaughter reached out to touch her hand.

"Cass… love… you're awake."

Cass groaned as a sharp pain wracked her body. "I tried to save him," she cried.

"You did save him, love," reassured her grandmother. "Typhoon, he's safe at Hope Bank."

146

"And Michael?"

Sarah Truman stared at her granddaughter, squeezing her hand, her expression vague. "Michael?"

"Michael Miller," insisted Cass. "It's him I have to save."

"There, there, now love, you're confused, that's all. The last time you had a fall from that crazy horse of yours you went on and on about saving Michael. That was then and this is now, it's different. Just lie back and relax, and I'll call the nurse."

Cass tried to sit up, the needle in her hand pulling against her skin. "What day is it?" she cried. "How long have I been out of it?"

Her grandmother stroked her head again, pressing her gently back down. "You *were* unconscious," she said. "But not for long, and when you did wake up the doctor gave you something to put you properly to sleep, so it's only been one night since your horrible accident – Oh Cass, you were so lucky. You could have been killed."

"How long, though?" begged Cass.

Sarah Truman glanced down at her watch. "Well, right now it's nine o'clock on the morning of Monday, the 30th of August."

The whole room began to swim, whirling around and around, white and green and silver, spiraling colors that sucked Cass in to a place where she really did not want to go.

Sarah's worried gaze settled upon her granddaughter's terrified face. "Why love, why do you ask? I already told you, your precious Typhoon is safely home at Hope Bank with the Ashtons. You're safe now, so just try to relax. Here, the nurse is here to see you, and she'll help."

Kind eyes, soft hands, a gentle murmuring voice and the overpowering smell of antiseptic evened out the swirling colors. The bright-faced nurse smiled and took Cass's arm.

"Sleep, young lady, that's what you need," she said, staring down at her with the calm professionalism that would still be there even if you were about to die. Was Michael about to die?

Cass hardly noticed the sting in her arm, for all she could see were Michael's dark eyes, Michael's body slumped at the bottom of the bank, the bank that she herself had just fallen down. "No!" She tried to sit up. "I have to save Michael."

As firm but gentle hands pressed her back down onto the bed the colors came back, spiraling out of control, smaller and smaller until they became a mere pinprick against the blackness that crept in all around her.

"How are you feeling now, love?" Sarah Truman stroked her granddaughter's brow, rocking slightly from side to side to ease her aching muscles. "Granddad Bill will be back soon, he's just run home to get me a change of clothes."

"What time is it?"

Cass's voice came out as a croak but she felt different now, more alert, and the pain had lessened.

"It's almost four o'clock. Are you hungry?"

Was she hungry? Cass licked her lips and her stomach gurgled. "Have you heard anything – is Michael all right?"

There was a trace of impatience in Sarah Truman's response. "Oh, no, not that again. Love, Michael is absolutely fine; it's yourself you should be worried about."

Cass heaved a sigh. It was late afternoon; she could see the sun through her window, already hanging low in the sky. It was over; surely it had to be over.

"Well, it's good to see you looking brighter," announced Bill Truman, filling the small room with his larger-than-life presence. "We'll have you home in no time."

Cass eased herself up onto her elbows, ignoring the pain brought on by even that small movement. "Is everything all right?" she asked eagerly.

He made a face, depositing a large bag onto the floor beside the bed. "Well, let me see; my granddaughter rode her crazy horse for miles yesterday and was almost killed when it fell down a bank with her, but otherwise... otherwise, I think things are just fine and dandy."

Cass sat up taller. "It wasn't Typhoon's fault," she insisted.

Her grandfather sat down on the side of the bed. "We know that, love. The truck driver came to see me today and he told me everything. The poor man was distraught. His boss came too, and he promised that after this they would no longer allow their drivers to use that road as a shortcut. He said the council will put up a No Access for Heavy Vehicles sign. Now how about that?"

Cass fell back on her pillows, a huge sense of release washing over her in a mind-blowing wave. She had done it, she really had changed fate. Michael was safe and her accident had stopped the trucks that might be a threat to him in the future.

"I want to go home," she whispered.

"And so you will," promised her grandmother. "The doctor said that you might even be well enough tomorrow, if you get enough rest, that is."

On the morning that Cass returned to Hope Bank the yard was quiet. It had been a whole week since she had come home from the hospital and a whole week since she had seen Typhoon... It seemed like a lifetime.

The Ashtons had been to see her, offering their condolences and promising to look after Ty and Sunny until she was well again, but she hadn't heard anything from Michael, except that he was safe and well, of course. Would he be here today she wondered, would he say anything? But what was there to say? It was over, and that was it. It was over.

The thought of riding Typhoon again filled her with both longing and dread, but when she actually saw him, it was as if nothing had ever happened. He looked at her with big bright interested eyes, tossing his lovely head in anticipation of some attention, and she hurriedly opened the stable door and slipped inside. His scent flooded her senses as she pressed her cheek against his silken neck, and he blew gently though his nostrils. Suddenly she realized that she was longing to ride him.

"It's over, boy," she murmured, stroking his velvety nose. "It really is over, and now we can both get on with our lives."

Michael arrived midmorning while Cass and Laura were sweeping the yard, grinning at them with his usual good humor. "Glad to see that you're out and about again, Cass," he called before disappearing into Robert's office to discuss which horses needed to be worked today. Cass felt a vague disappointment lodge itself securely in her throat.

"Right," announced Laura. "I'm going to fetch Marius in from the paddock. Will you be okay?"

Cass flashed her a smile. "Of course, I'm fine. You don't need to look after me."

She was busy grooming Typhoon, taking delight in bringing a gleam to the horse's black satin coat, when Michael came to find her.

A shadow fell across the stable and she lowered her body brush, looking over to see his tall shape in the doorway, blocking out the sunshine. She couldn't see the expression on his face as he walked toward her.

"It was meant for me, wasn't it?"

Cass placed her brush back down into the grooming box with careful deliberation, trembling deep inside. "What do you mean?"

"Your accident. It was the one you tried to warn me about."

She dared herself to meet his eyes and left them resting on the line of his jaw. "In my dream, or whatever it was, it happened to you on August 30th... but you didn't walk away."

He reached out to touch her arm. "I did ride that way that same day, but, thanks to you, there were no trucks."

Cass grinned, a lighthearted euphoria flooding her veins as her eyes finally moved up to meet his. "Then maybe I really did save your life."

"Ah, but maybe it was Typhoon?" he responded. "Maybe my dad was right about him all along, and he really can see things that others can't. After all, Tempest is his twin. Maybe Ty just passed his vision on to you."

He smiled then, his dark eyes crinkling at the corners. Was he just laughing at her, Cass wondered, or did he really believe that there was some truth to all of this?

"Well, I suppose we'll never know for sure, will we?" she sighed, looking across to where the gleaming black gelding stood stock still, ears pricked, staring toward the horizon with a distant expression in his shining dark eyes. "I wonder what he's thinking now?"

When Michael curled his fingers around hers she shivered deep inside.

"Well, I know what I'm thinking," he murmured, pulling her around to face him.

151